What the press say of Harlequin Romances...

OTHER
Harlequin Romances
by MARGARET MAYO

Rainbow Magic

by

MARGARET MAYO

Harlequin Books

TORONTO • LONDON • NEW YORK • AMSTERDAM • SYDNEY

Original hardcover edition published in 1977
by Mills & Boon Limited

ISBN 0-373-02086-4

Harlequin edition published July 1977

Printed in U.S.A.

CHAPTER ONE

TARYN dug in her heels and urged Dainty into a gallop. Her corn-cold hair flew out behind and she laughed aloud in sheer enjoyment. Out here on the moors the wind had whipped a healthy colour into her cheeks and she looked a different person from the heartbroken girl who had returned home several months ago.

She was oblivious to the sudden sharp shower that speckled her yellow shirt in darkening spots, aware only of a feeling of freedom and wondering why she had never sought to escape this peaceful corner of England.

Her sorrel horse took the incline in his stride, not hesitating until he reached the brow of the hill. Here horse and rider were silhouetted against the sky. The ground levelled out again before dropping sharply into a valley and from force of habit the animal slowed and stopped, knowing that his owner liked to pause a while in this spot.

From this vantage point the village of Ferndale could clearly be seen, but it was not the cottages that drew Taryn's attention this day, nor the meandering stream that disappeared underground before emerging many miles later to open out into the sea. It was the large house to her right built high on the western slopes. Austere and forbidding, Dale End had lain empty for many years, a sentinel over the valley.

But now it had a new owner. Tomorrow he was visiting the place to decide exactly how much work needed doing to make it habitable. Curiosity in the village was rife, but Taryn had more than just normal interest—she hoped to get a job there. In actual fact an interview had been arranged for the next morning.

The shower had passed and the warm summer sun was already drying Taryn's clothes. As she looked across the valley a rainbow appeared—faintly at first but soon deepening into a colourful prismatic arch. It was not the rainbow itself that drew forth a surprised cry from Taryn's lips and made her sit forward in her saddle, but the fact that it formed a perfect bridge from east to west—one end disappearing into the woodland above and beyond the village and the other appearing to touch Dale End itself.

How many times as a child had she prayed to find a rainbow like this? Of course, she was too old now for such fantasies, but she could not help recalling Great-Aunt Margaret's prophecy that whenever a rainbow spanned the valley in just this position a dramatic change was about to take place in the life of the beholder. The last time this natural phenomenon had occurred her father had been a young man. Standing in this precise spot, he had shortly afterwards met and fallen in love with her mother. Taryn had argued that the meeting would have taken place anyway, but Great-Aunt Margaret had been adamant that the rainbow had influenced their encounter.

Despite the fact that she scoffed at this theory Taryn could not help feeling excited. Even Dainty stood unusually still, his ears alerted as though he too was impressed by this astounding sight. It was not until the noise increased that she realised it was an approaching aircraft that attracted his attention. She watched as it cut through the coloured arc. At closer quarters she saw it was a helicopter—a huge white mechanical bird. Three times it circled the valley before swooping suddenly in the direction of the girl on horseback. She watched in total fascination, not really believing that he was going to land here; but as the characteristic drone grew louder, joined now by the whirr of the rotating blades, she was left in no doubt as to the pilot's intention.

Before she had time to goad Dainty into action a strong current of air rushed across the clearing, tugging at her hair and clothes and causing her breath to catch in her throat. The grass and shrub were whipped into a frenzy as though by a whirlwind. The horse reared in fright, catching Taryn unawares. She made a futile grab for the reins before feeling herself fly through the air to land with a force that took all the breath from her body. The noise was now deafening. She attempted to rise, but, temporarily winded, could do no more than lift her head. The great white machine hovered ominously near and she closed her eyes and buried her face in the turf, confident that it was only a matter of seconds before she would be crushed.

Suddenly all was still once again. Taryn rolled over as a shadow crossed her body. She looked up at the tall figure, then shook her head in disbelief. It couldn't be! He had always said he would never return to England. What was he doing here now? 'Mark!' Her lips formed the word, though no sound came. Slowly she rose to her feet and stood facing the man who had once meant so much to her—and now —what did she feel now? Anger! A sudden searing anger that he had the nerve to seek her out again after all that had happened. Hadn't he done enough damage without reopening the wound?

'What the devil do you think you're playing at?' He spoke first. 'Why didn't you move?'

He was still the same arrogant brute. Why had she ever thought herself in love with him? The answer was simple. When she was alone in a strange country he had befriended her. He was fiendishly handsome and could be perfectly charming when he tried. She looked into the tawny eyes, hard now and calculating—so different from their velvet softness in one of his more tender moods. His full lips were drawn into a tight line as he waited for her reply.

'I could ask what you're doing here,' she returned. 'Don't you think you've hurt me enough?'

He frowned. 'What do you mean—hurt you?'

'Either you have a very short memory, Mark Vandyke, or you're being deliberately evasive.' Taryn held herself stiffly, proudly, her eyes meeting and holding those of the dark, handsome man who had appeared so suddenly and incredibly on the scene.

He gave a short laugh. 'I think there's been some

mistake. My name's not Mark Vandyke.'

'But——' she stared uncomprehendingly, 'but you must be. You can't tell me I don't know the man I was going to marry. What game are you playing?'

He ran fingers through his short brown hair, an expression of amused bewilderment crossing his face. 'I'm sorry to disappoint you.' His eyes ran appraisingly over her slim, taut figure in the close-fitting shirt and faded blue jeans. 'Even more sorry that I'm *not* your young man.'

'I doubt it, if you knew how I felt,' snapped Taryn. 'I never want to see him again as long as I live. But if you're not Mark, then who are you, and what are you doing here?'

'I think that's my business,' he returned blandly.

'In that case,' turning away, 'I'll go and find my horse.'

His eyebrows slid up. 'If you don't know how to control the animal you shouldn't ride him.'

Taryn glared. 'Dainty is most obedient. It's just that he's not used to being nearly blown off his feet by some huge mechanical monster coming down out of the sky.'

He seemed unperturbed by her outburst. 'You'll probably find he's gone home. I should try there first.'

'Naturally.' She flung him one last scathing glance before swinging sharply away. She still could not really believe he was not Mark, yet he had seemed genuine enough in his denial of the other man's identity.

Taryn sensed him watching her, but refused to

give him the satisfaction of turning round. Head held high, she tramped the half mile or so back to the hamlet, her mind in a turmoil and her serenity of the morning rudely disturbed. It was uncanny that two men should so closely resemble each other; even his voice held the same inflections. She shivered despite the warmth of the day; the unhappy memories she was striving so hard to forget flooding again to the forefront of her mind.

Mark! The man to whom she had lost her heart. The first and only time she had been in love. She grimaced wryly. How he must have laughed behind her back. So often he had said he had business to attend to when all the while it had been Maria. *Maria!* She said the name aloud in loathing and disgust.

She reached the row of cottages and there, in the field opposite where he was kept during the summer months, stood Dainty, looking not in the least concerned and none the worse for his fright. Taryn stopped to speak encouragingly to him, a little annoyed that the stranger had been right, before entering the cottage she shared with Great-Aunt Margaret.

Gammy, as she was fondly called by one and all, was in the kitchen preparing tea. A widow in her mid-fifties, she still bore on her face the tell-tale lines of grief etched there following the tragic death of her husband in the same car accident that had killed Taryn's parents six years ago. She had blamed herself for letting them go, having foreseen that something evil was going to happen that day. Gammy's premonitions were an expected part of family life, and as Taryn looked upon the woman who had become her second mother she suddenly remembered the rainbow. Her meeting with the man in the helicopter had pushed it from her mind.

'Gammy,' she said, her face alight with excitement, 'did you see the rainbow?'

Her aunt turned from the sandwich she was making, her startling blue eyes observing Taryn keenly. They were very much alike, both with the same fine bone structure as had all the women in the Penreath family, but whereas Taryn's hair was the colour of ripened corn, Margaret's was dark brown, peppered now with white, which instead of making her look older only served to enhance the woman's basic beauty. 'I've been too busy to notice the weather, but judging by the look on your face this was no ordinary rainbow.'

'It wasn't. It wasn't. Oh, Gammy, I've seen *the* rainbow!' She might have been back in her infancy when all the children used to look for Gammy's special rainbow.

Gammy smiled indulgently. 'I knew you would one day, Taryn, it was in your stars. You can forget your broken heart now. All will be well. No one has ever had bad luck after seeing that rainbow.'

'I'd like to believe you, Gammy dear.' Taryn pulled out a kitchen chair from beneath the table and turning it round sat astride, her arms resting along the back, her chin on her hands. 'But I think you're wrong this time. In fact, I *know* you are.'

'How can you say that? You've hardly given it time.'

Taryn pulled a face. 'You'll never believe me—but only seconds after I saw the rainbow a helicopter landed in the top field. It scared poor Dainty half out of his wits. He threw me and bolted for home. I don't mind admitting for a minute I thought I was going to be crushed beneath it.'

Gammy frowned and put down the knife. 'That's strange, but I shouldn't let it worry you. Who was it? Do you know?'

'If you think that's strange, wait till you hear the rest.' Taryn paused to get the greater effect from her words. 'It was Mark!'

Gammy snorted in disbelief. 'Of all the nerve! What did *he* want? He'd better not——'

'Wait,' chuckled Taryn. 'I *thought* it was Mark, he looked like him—and he spoke like him—but when I asked him why he was here he didn't know what I was talking about. He didn't know me, and the name Mark Vandyke meant nothing to him.'

'Are you sure?' more puzzled now than before.

'Positive. He wouldn't tell me who he was, but honestly, Gammy, I'd be willing to stake my life that it's Mark.'

Taryn's aunt sank on to a chair and passed a hand over her forehead. 'I can't take this in. If it is Mark why did he lie to you? Did he look ill? Perhaps he's suffering from amnesia?'

'I never thought of that, but—no, I don't think so. He was a picture of health; in fact I've never seen him look fitter.' It was one solution, though. If he had lost his memory it would certainly account for the way he behaved. Many was the time she had told

12

him about the village where she had spent her childhood. Perhaps some chord of his memory still retained her vivid descriptions of this Devonshire village. Maybe Ferndale was the only name he could recall and he was trying to evoke more memories by visiting it?

'Why didn't you bring him here?' asked Gammy next. 'I should like to see this young man about whom I've heard so much.'

Taryn sniffed. 'Our meeting hardly warranted invitations. He wasn't very friendly.'

'I doubt if you gave him the opportunity. Knowing how you feel about Mark I can imagine your reaction.'

'Especially when he nearly killed me!'

'Don't exaggerate, Taryn.'

'But he did. Another few inches and it would have been all over.'

'Inches?' meaningly.

'Well—yards perhaps, but it was too close for my liking.'

Just then the door burst open and young Rory, Taryn's seven-year-old nephew, dashed in, his eyes shining and blond curls bobbing. 'Gammy, Aunty Taryn, have you seen the helicopter? I asked the man if I could have a ride and he said he'll take me up tomorrow.'

'You'll do no such thing,' burst out Taryn, horrified. 'Don't you know better than to speak to strangers?' Especially this one, she added to herself.

'Yes—but he's different.' The boy looked crestfallen. 'You don't really mean it, Aunty Taryn?

He's ever so nice and he didn't seem to mind me asking.'

'I do mean it,' said Taryn, 'and when your father finds out I expect he'll say the same. Did this man tell you who he was and what he was doing here?' She had not meant to ask these questions, they slipped out without her thinking.

Rory shook his head sadly. 'Mummy was calling me, I had to come away.'

'What did she say about you talking to this man?' asked Gammy.

'She doesn't know.'

'Because you knew she wouldn't approve.' Gammy handed him a fruit scone. 'You'd better run back home and if I were you I'd forget all about your promised ride.'

As if by mutual consent no further mention was made of the man who resembled Mark Vandyke. After tea Taryn and her aunt spent some time in the garden, then as dusk was falling the girl said she felt tired and was going to bed.

From her bedroom window, if she leaned right out, Taryn could just make out the outline of the helicopter standing on the brow of the hill. So he was still here! She could not help but wonder where he was staying and what reason he had for visiting Ferndale. And more important still, was he really Mark?

She undressed in the dark in her tiny room under the eaves of Honeysuckle Cottage. Why had this man come? Why had he spoilt the happiness it had taken her so long to recapture? Just twelve months ago she had been on the verge of a promising career. After two years at college she had been all set to become a fabric designer in one of Italy's leading fashion houses. Her meeting with Mark had only added to her happiness. The future had never looked rosier. Then suddenly it was all over. She was left with a broken heart and the desire to leave Naples. To return once again to the place of her birth; to the family who would give her the love and affection she needed; the consolation to carry her through the following months.

It had not been easy, but with the help of Gammy, her brother, Robert, and other friends and relations who lived in this close-knit community she had at last succeeded in forgetting Mark. It was only on very rare occasions that he sprang to mind, when an action or a deed reminded her of him. But now she felt the old misery seeping back. She climbed into bed and buried her face in the pillow. Who was he? Why had he come? And if it was Mark why didn't he know her?

Surprisingly Taryn drifted into unconsciousness within a few minutes, not waking until half past seven the next morning. Through her window she could see Dale End high on the opposite side of the valley. The early morning sun picked out its crumbling stones and tried unsuccessfully to reflect in the mullioned windows, made dull by the storms it had weathered over the last decade. Her heart skipped a beat. Today—for the first time—she would be entering the house. It would take much work to put it to rights, but the challenge was inviting. She hoped she would be successful in getting the job of interior designer. It was not exactly what she had been trained for, but with her eye for colour and design she could foresee no difficulties. She felt quite excited at the prospect and hurriedly washed and dressed and went downstairs where Gammy was already preparing breakfast, her unhappiness of last night temporarily forgotten.

'I'm pleased to see you looking more cheerful this morning,' greeted her aunt, then glancing at the girl's trousers and shirt, 'You're not going for your interview dressed like that?'

'Why not?' Taryn looked down at her red trousers and white top. 'I thought they looked rather elegant. They are new.'

'Don't you think a dress would be more suitable?' Gammy still looked doubtful.

'I feel comfortable in trousers,' returned Taryn. 'Besides, they're more practical.'

'I don't want you jeopardising your chances of this job. I know how much you're looking forward to it.'

'Really, Gammy,' laughed Taryn, 'I can't see that it makes any difference what I wear. It's my abilities the man's interested in.'

It seemed the whole village knew she was going for an interview this morning. As she walked past the row of stone cottages, each with their painted walls and thatched roofs, she received all sorts of well wishes. It was not until she saw Robert with young Rory in tow that she recalled her encounter of the previous day. Looking ahead towards the end of the valley she saw the helicopter still silhouetted against the skyline.

Robert followed her line of vision. 'I hear that you too have met our mysterious visitor?' As fair as his sister and with the same blue eyes, he looked at her in amusement.

'How do you know?' she asked quickly.

'Gammy was at Gran's last night, and I heard her say that you'd met a man you thought was Mark. Say, Sis, was it really him? I've been dying to meet him. I want to see if he lives up to my impression of a fashion designer.'

'And what might that be, pray?' lifting her chin and trying to look dignified.

'You know—like this,' and he affected an exaggerated walk with his hand on his hip, turning back to look at her. 'How am I doing?'

She was forced to laugh. 'You're impossible, Rob! If you must know he was nothing like that. He has a marvellous physique, more like an athlete than anything else. We'd have made a great team, had things been different.'

'You never told me what really happened. All I know is that you came home looking as though the world had crashed about your ears.'

'I still prefer not to discuss it,' said Taryn quietly. 'Yesterday I might have done, but now—it's all so real again.'

'And you think this fellow,' looking again towards the aircraft, 'might be Mark? Gammy said that perhaps he'd lost his memory, but if he had he's hardly likely to come here. No one's ever heard of Ferndale.

17

It's not even on the map. It's too much of a coincidence.'

'My feelings exactly,' sighed Taryn, 'but if it's not him then who is it? The similarity is frightening.'

She looked so upset that he put his arm about her shoulders and gave her a comforting hug. 'Don't worry, Sis, big brother will look after you. I must scoot now or Rory will be late for school. Best of luck with the interview. Let me know how you get on.'

Taryn had intended walking along the road that led out of the valley and back across the top of the hill to Dale End, but her talk with Robert had held her up. Unless she wanted to be late she would have to scramble up the hillside. She crossed the tiny bridge over the stream and began her climb. There had once been a path of sorts, but through years of disuse it had become overgrown with grasses and ferns—from which the valley had been given its name—and Taryn had difficulty in finding her way.

In one particularly steep part she missed her footing altogether and slid back several yards. The ground was dry, but even so she was horrified to find grass stains on the knees of her once immaculate trousers and a tiny tear in the sleeve of her blouse where it had caught on a blackberry bush. Her hands too suffered in the attempt to save herself and by the time she reached the grounds of Dale End she was conscious of looking more than a little dishevelled. She rubbed her hands on the seat of her pants in an endeavour to clean them and searched her handbag in vain for a comb.

As she picked her way through the wilderness of garden Taryn looked up at the house. It had been many years since she had seen it at such close quarters. The previous owner had been a recluse who chased off inquisitive children who ventured too near. It was said that he kept a rifle ready for anyone who did not heed his warnings—though Taryn could not recall there ever having been any foundation for this story. Nevertheless it was deterrent enough to keep the villagers away, and even though the house had now stood empty for so long no one ever dared to go near for fear the ghost of old Henry—as he was called—had returned to guard his property.

No doubt it was this tale of it being haunted that had scared off any prospective purchasers in the past, for there had been much interest shown in the house, but now Taryn looked forward to meeting the man who had scoffed at such stories. She only hoped that he would not hold her appearance against her.

Built of local grey stone, Dale End stood tall and impressive. It was almost like a castle, thought Taryn, noting the crenellated towers at each corner. A crumbling portico ran the length of the building where wild roses had taken the opportunity of time to build up a dense barrier against the outside world. They had recently been hacked away round the entrance to the front door, and not stopping to stare any longer Taryn mounted the steps and raised the heavy knocker, which was moulded in the shape of a lion's head. It echoed throughout the empty house before dying away into silence. For a moment she thought there was no one inside until at last she heard footsteps approaching. The door swung noisily open, and Taryn assumed her brightest smile. 'Good morning, I'm——' Her words died on her lips. Her face blanched. 'Oh, no! Not you!'

The dark man's face altered noticeably. His eyes narrowed and hardened. 'I'm equally surprised, but I hope not as rude. Please come in, Miss—er—Penreath.'

'I'm sorry,' she said quickly. 'I didn't mean to sound offensive.' Face to face again with the man who looked so like Mark, she clenched her fists in an effort to still her agitation. It was gloomy in the big house. The entrance hall in which she found herself was dank and cold. The one window set high in the wall above the door let in little light and the dark walls did not help. Suddenly she wished she had not come. She knew nothing about this man, apart from his startling resemblance to her one-time fiancé. If he was Mark what had happened to make him like this—and if he wasn't, who was he?

'I take it you *are* Miss Penreath?' he asked, looking quizzically at her tumbled hair and soiled clothing.

She felt herself grow hot under his gaze and moved uncomfortably. 'That's right, Taryn Penreath. I apologise for my appearance. I—I had a slight accident on the way here.'

His thick brows rose expressively. 'You'll do—for now. In actual fact I prefer to see a woman in something a little more feminine.'

'In a skirt, you mean,' Taryn returned tartly. 'In that case I won't waste your time any longer. Living in the country I find it more convenient to wear trousers. Being a man you wouldn't understand.'

'Oh, but I do.' He studied her insolently from head to toe. 'Also, being a man, I'm sure you must have a pair of shapely legs under those pants. It would be such a pity not to show them off.'

'How dare you!' Mark would never have spoken to her like that, even if he'd thought along the same lines. 'Mr Major, I think you're being very impertinent. After all, we hardly know each other.' She no longer cared that she was here to be interviewed for a job. If it meant working for this man she did not want it anyway.

'You seemed to think you knew me when we met yesterday.' He thrust his hands into his pockets and gave a crooked smile. 'Mark, did you call me?'

Taryn glared. 'It seems I was mistaken. Mark would never treat me like this.'

'I rather gained the impression that you and he were no longer friends?'

'We're not. That's why I would find it impossible to work for you, Mr Major. You'd only bring back unhappy memories.'

He tilted his head, regarding her with some amusement. 'Don't you think you're being rather hasty? Wait until you've seen what the job's all about. You might find it will more than make up for my unfortunate likeness to your ill-favoured boy-friend.'

She lifted her shoulders. 'Very well, though I'm sure I shan't change my mind.'

'It's a woman's prerogative, don't forget. Shall we start down here? I'm afraid there's no electricity yet and the windows don't let in much light, but it will give you a good idea of the general layout of the house. Then maybe you'll be able to think about it and come up with a few ideas. I'm no good at this sort of thing myself.'

Taryn followed him through one of the many doors leading from the hall. She stared at his broad back. He was *so* like Mark. How could she work for him without involving herself in more heartache? Even now memories were returning—in particular the night Mark had proposed. He had taken her to one of Naples' top restaurants. They had eaten oysters and drunk champagne and afterwards gone for a drive in his open-topped car. They had driven on to a beach, she couldn't remember where, and he had slipped the biggest diamond ring she had ever seen on to her finger. She had been deliriously happy.

'I thought I would have this room as my study. Are you listening?'

She was brought back to the present with a start. 'I'm sorry—I—I was thinking.'

'About Mark?' with a sudden frown.

Taryn nodded.

'I can see I'm going to have to learn to live with this counterpart of mine. Don't you think you're being somewhat foolish if it's all over between you?'

'How can I help it,' she responded, 'when you remind me of him?'

'Perhaps I ought to grow a beard,' stroking his freshly shaven chin.

Taryn saw the humour in his eyes and knew that he mocked her. But it was impossible not to feel as she did. Perhaps after a while, if she did take the job, she would become accustomed to seeing Mark's double, but at the moment it was impossible not to be flooded by memories.

With fresh determination she pulled a notebook from her bag. 'You were saying?'

He followed her lead. 'This would make a good study, don't you think? It has an excellent view over the valley.' The window opened protestingly at his touch and they looked out together. Taryn could see the row of tiny cottages which constituted the village. Gammy, looking like a doll from this height, working again in her garden; Janice polishing the windows; Robert, now back from taking Rory to school, fiddling about with his car. A typical scene in the life of the village, yet Taryn realised that once Luke Major was installed they would have little privacy. He would look down on them without their knowledge. Up till now they had been one big happy family. No outsiders had ever intruded into their lives. She was not sure that she liked the idea of a stranger invading their territory. But there was nothing she could do about it.

She made a few notes. 'Have you any preference regarding colour and style, Mr Major?'

'Luke, please, I can't stand formality.'

'Very well—Luke. Am I to be given a free rein?'

'I don't like modern stuff,' he said, 'but then I'm sure you'd never dream of suggesting anything like that. It would look so out of place in this house. I wonder why it's stood empty for so long?'

Taryn smiled. 'Haven't you heard? It's reputed

23

to be haunted—by the previous owner.'

'How interesting.' He seemed not in the least per-turbed. 'I've always wanted to meet a ghost.'

'You wouldn't be frightened?' asked Taryn, wide-eyed.

'Of course not. Ghosts can do no harm.'

'Well, I don't mind admitting that if I see one here I shall be off as quick as a shot, and I shan't come back again.'

'Then you've decided to take the job?' he asked quickly.

'Not yet. Shall we move on?'

'Why, I do believe you're scared. Surely you don't believe all those old tales?' He was openly laughing at her, but as they moved into the next room he pulled her hand through his arm. 'You're cold. Let's hurry up and get finished so that we can go out into the warm sunshine.'

She was enchanted by the house and already had visions of what it might look like. Small bedrooms converted into bathrooms; woodwork stripped down to its natural colour. The whole house had a grace, a nobility, longing to be released. She could imagine it restored to its former elegant glory and felt an excitement in the challenge. It was different from any work she had ever done before, but she knew she could do it. Her eyes shone as she worked out colour schemes and she hurried from room to room, ex-claiming over Adam fireplaces and baroque carvings.

At last they returned to the hall. 'Well,' said Luke, 'need I ask whether you've changed your mind? One look at your face tells me that you're entranced

24

by the prospect, and on my part I know I'll not be disappointed. Have you done much of this sort of work?'

Taryn's heart dropped. 'Why, no. But I thought you knew. I was a fabric designer. I can do it, though, really I can. I can see it all now. We'll have a——'

He held up his hand. 'Wait a moment! Don't get carried away. It matters not in the least what you've done before. I know instinctively that you'll make a good job of my house. I shall look forward to seeing the results of your labours.'

Taryn didn't know whether to be pleased or not. She was delighted at the prospect of designing the decor for Dale End, but did she really want to work in such close proximity with a man who looked so like Mark? Over the last few months she had grown very bitter towards the man who had thrown her over for another woman. Would she be able to forget Mark and treat Luke as a separate individual? It was so easy to link the two together. Mark and Luke. Luke and Mark. It was unbelievable that two people should be so alike. Perhaps Gammy had guessed correctly and it was Mark suffering from amnesia. There was a subtle difference in his character, but wouldn't an accident resulting in loss of memory cause such a change?

If only she could find out something about Luke's background! So far he had not mentioned himself at all—whether he had a wife—and family—or why he had chosen to make Dale End his home. All she could do was wait until he volunteered some information. Wait and watch. She herself had known Mark so intimately that surely he would give himself away if he was the same man. But it would be strange working with Luke, wondering all the time whether she had once lain in his arms, whether it was his kisses that had aroused her to the heights of passion—and whether it was this same man who had subsequently broken her heart, resulting in bitter disillusionment and the wish never to see him again. It would be difficult to hold back her resentment.

'You're very quiet. Have you any doubts?'

'I was wondering if it would work out. I might forget you're not Mark and——'

'I don't think you need have any fears there,' he broke in. 'I shan't be here all of the time. I'm sending someone over tomorrow and I want you to go over the plans with him; explain exactly what you have in mind. It won't be too soon?'

Taryn shook her head. 'I've already got a good idea of what wants doing, and I have the rest of the day to mull it over and get it down on paper.'

'That's settled, then.' He touched her shoulder briefly and flashed one of his uneven smiles. His eyes in the dim light of the hall were unfathomable, deep and dark as a night sky, and Taryn turned away quickly. Memories were still too near the surface.

'Now we've finished how about inviting me back for a cup of tea? I'm afraid facilities here are sadly lacking at the moment.'

Taryn shot him a startled glance. 'You'll find the cottage I share with my great-aunt rather cramped compared with this.' Besides which she did not relish the idea of his accompanying her back through the village. There was already enough curiosity about the man who was buying Dale End without her being seen taking him home.

'I'm not proud,' he said. 'I was brought up in a village myself. Some of my happiest memories belong there.'

'In that case,' she replied, 'I'm sure Gammy won't mind.'

He opened the door and stood back for her to pass. The sunshine outside seemed warm and safe and suddenly Taryn felt much happier. It was unfair of her to treat Luke Major in any other way than in the friendly manner he extended towards her. She smiled as they walked along the overgrown path. It was almost like her first meeting with Mark all over again. Only this time she must not fall in love!

CHAPTER TWO

As Taryn had anticipated, Gammy was delighted to meet the new owner of Dale End, and Luke in his turn further won her approval by declaring she looked too young to be Taryn's great-aunt.

'You flatter me, young man,' she said, 'but I won't pretend I don't like it. Do take off your coat and make yourself at home. Taryn will keep you entertained while I make a pot of tea.'

But Taryn had just caught a horrified glimpse of herself in the mirror. Her normally sleek hair was windswept and bedraggled and there was a smut on her nose. Together with her torn clothing she looked a sorry sight. She went hot at the thought that she had spent the last two hours in Luke's company looking like this. In fact she was surprised he had decided to give her the job, for she was nothing like the impression she had tried to create of a responsible young woman who knew exactly what she was doing.

'I'm sorry,' she said quickly, trying to smooth her hair with a hasty dab of her hand, 'but I must wash and change. I didn't realise I——'

'That's quite all right,' interposed Luke with a grin. 'I'll go and give Gammy my moral support. Take as long as you like.'

He hung his coat over the back of a chair and followed her aunt from the room. Taryn shrugged and climbed the narrow stairs which led up from the living room. It did not take long to wash off the tell-tale stains of her climb up to Dale End. Contemplating her reflection in the bathroom mirror, she was surprised to see a new glow to her face. In the months since her broken love affair she had felt—and looked—listless and tired. Her eyes had lacked their customary sparkle. But now, suddenly and without warning, it was back. She put up her hands to suddenly hot cheeks. Please don't let me be taken in again, she prayed silently, and then scolded herself for being silly. Luke meant nothing to her. If anything she hated him for reminding her so much of Mark. It was the thought of the job, the new challenge, that had done this to her. It was nothing to do with the man for whom she would be working.

In her bedroom she studied the contents of the small wardrobe. She had half pulled out a dress before thrusting it back with a gesture of impatience. She could imagine Luke's reaction and she certainly wasn't going to give him the pleasure of thinking she had dressed just to please him. Finally she tugged on a pair of clean jeans and a check shirt, brushed her shoulder-length hair until it shone, and satisfied that she looked presentable, if not ladylike, went back downstairs.

Tea was made and Luke occupied one of the chintz-covered fireside chairs. Gammy presided over the teapot and Taryn was forced to take the other chair on the opposite side of the hearth. She pretended not to notice the way Luke eyed her up and down, though she knew exactly what he was thinking.

'What have you been saying to your aunt?' he asked. 'She seems under the impression that I'm your Mark Vandyke suffering from amnesia.'

'Gammy!' Taryn shot the older woman a scandalised glance.

'It's true,' she protested, not looking in the least concerned, 'You said yourself that you thought he was Mark. I'm just trying to find out the truth.'

'Well, I can tell you both here and now,' he said, 'that I am not Mark Vandyke. My name is Luke Major—always has been and always will be. Now are you satisfied?' His eyes held a gleam of suppressed laughter.

'I have no alternative,' returned Taryn, 'but I can't help feeling it strange that two men should look so completely alike.' Disconcerting too, she thought, especially when seen in such close proximity.

'Have you no brothers?' asked Gammy as she handed Luke his tea. 'Could it be that Taryn's friend is related?'

'Thank you.' He took a sip of the steaming liquid before answering. 'Sorry to disappoint you again,' he drawled at last, 'I'm an only child. I don't even boast a cousin.'

'How strange,' murmured Gammy, absently stirring her tea. 'Of course, I've never met Mark, but Taryn was so sure.'

'You both seem very disturbed that I'm not the man you think I am. He seems to have had a profound effect on your lives.'

'You don't forget a man who's broken your heart,' returned Taryn hastily. 'Now if you don't mind changing the subject, I'm a little sick and tired of hearing about him.'

'If you'd rather I went——' he said, beginning to rise.

'You'll do no such thing,' protested Gammy. 'I'm ashamed of you, Taryn! Where are your manners?'

'I'm sorry,' she mumbled, avoiding Luke's eyes. 'I can't help how I feel.'

Gammy spoke again. 'I've a very nice piece of lamb for lunch, Mr Major, if you'd like to stay?'

'How kind of you. I'd be delighted—provided your great-niece has no objection?'

'Would it matter if I had?' asked Taryn with some asperity. He had spoken lightly, but she felt suddenly disgruntled by the apparent ease with which he had made friends with Gammy. Couldn't her aunt see that by encouraging him she was only making things worse for Taryn herself?

'Taryn!' exclaimed the older woman in shocked tones.

But Luke merely smiled, his eyes sardonically mocking her. 'Not really, since the invitation came from your gracious aunt.'

'In that case,' she returned, 'please be our guest.'

He passed back his empty cup. 'There's just one thing, Gammy—I may call you that?'

'Please do,' beaming her pleasure.

'I must leave at two. I have important business this afternoon.'

'Then I'll go and see to it at once.' She stacked the empty cups on the tray, her best rose china ones, observed Taryn, only brought out for special visitors,

31

and disappeared into the adjoining kitchen.

'I'll come and help,' volunteered Taryn, preparing to rise.

'No need,' called her aunt over her shoulder. 'You stay and keep our visitor company. Show him the garden if you like.'

Taryn looked across at Luke, her fine brows raised expressively. 'It's Gammy's pride and joy, but I'm sure you won't be interested.'

'On the contrary, I'd be delighted. I miss a garden, living in a flat. I remember when I was a boy my mother gave me my own little patch. I was so proud of the first flowers I grew. I don't think anything compares with the first time you do something, whether it's the first flowers you've grown; the first time you're allowed out alone; your first kiss; the first time you fall in love.'

He watched closely for her reaction. Taryn felt sure he was trying to find out more about her affair with Mark. Why else would he reminisce like this? Men weren't usually so nostalgic.

She smiled briefly and pushed herself up from the chair. If he thought she was going to make any comment he would be disappointed.

Outside she felt easier. In the tiny room his presence had been overpowering, but now she breathed in the warm June air and relaxed. 'There's not much to see.' She sounded apologetic as he followed her along the narrow path between two strips of smooth green lawn.

But the profusion of colour here was a pleasure to the most unappreciative eye. It was a typical cottage garden—flowers of every sort vying with each other for attention. They passed between clumps of holly-hocks, where the bees were busy at work; giant sun-flowers nodded their heads in greeting; the humble marigold encroached across the path defying to be overlooked; lupins, delphiniums, pyrethrums, all mingled happily together. Occasionally Luke would stop and bend his head to appreciate the particular scent of one flower.

If she had not been sure before Taryn could be now that this man was not Mark. She could never imagine Mark actually enjoying the sounds and smells of a country garden. His work was his life and nothing had ever been allowed to interrupt it—until the coming of Maria! The only flowers in which he was interested were orchids or other exotic blooms with which to enhance his creations.

She had not realised she was staring until Luke spoke. 'Is something the matter? You're looking at me very strangely. Don't say you're still comparing me with Mark?'

He was so near to the truth that Taryn flushed, but she was spared the humility of answering by a tiny voice calling from behind the fuchsia hedge.

'Aunty Taryn, Aunty Taryn! Guess what we did at school! I——' Rory stopped when he saw she was not alone. He looked questioningly at Luke before breaking out into a grin. 'You're the helicopter man!' and then accusingly to Taryn, 'You didn't tell me you knew him. Why did you say I couldn't go for a ride?'

Feeling Luke's swift glance in her direction, Taryn spoke softly to the boy. 'Because I know what's best

33

for you. Mr Major hasn't time to take little boys for joy-rides.'

'Let me answer that one for myself,' interrupted her companion. 'I said I'd give you a ride and so I will.'

'Gee, thanks, Mr Major.' Rory hopped up and down excitedly, while looking hopefully at Taryn from beneath fair lashes.

She turned her attention to Luke. 'He didn't know you,' she protested. 'He should have known better than to talk to strangers.'

'But he's not a stranger any more, so it's all right now, isn't it, Aunty Taryn?' Rory tugged her hand impatiently.

As usual Luke appeared amused by her indecision. 'I suppose so,' she said reluctantly. 'If Mr Major's sure it's no trouble.'

'Mr Major's quite sure,' mimicked Luke softly. He held out his hand. 'Come along, young man. There's no time like the present.'

Readily Rory slipped his hand into Luke's.

'I think you ought to ask your mother first,' suggested Taryn. 'Your dinner must be nearly ready.'

'Take me to her,' commanded Luke with a smile. 'I'll ask the good lady myself,' and then in a conspiratorial whisper to Rory, 'I'm sure she won't say no to me.'

Taryn watched them go, man and boy, laughing together over something Luke had said. She envied Rory his childhood innocence, his ability for instant friendship without any of the inhibitions he would feel in later life. It was not until you had been hurt that you learned to distrust, she thought. Until her meeting with Mark she had been as innocent and vulnerable as her nephew. None of life's harsh realities had marred her path. That was why her grief had been doubly hard to bear. No one had prepared her for such trials.

Sighing deeply and despising herself for allowing the past once again to catch up with her, she retraced her steps into the house.

Gammy looked up, surprised to see her alone. 'Where's Luke?'

'Taking Rory up in his helicopter. I hope they won't be long. I should hate him to be late back at school.'

Her aunt laughed. 'So the little one's got his way after all. Stir this gravy for me, there's a love, while I slice the meat. Your new employer must be very rich—buying a big house like Dale End *and* owning a helicopter.'

'How do you know it's his?'

'Because I asked him. He's got his own business too.'

'Gammy!' Taryn was horrified. 'How could you?'

Aunt Margaret gave a satisfied smile. 'I wanted to know what sort of a man my favourite niece is going to work for. You can't be too careful these days.'

Taryn felt annoyed and pleased both at the same time. 'And does he pass?' she asked drily.

'He's a nice boy,' her aunt said. 'I have no fears there. If your Mark was anything like him I can see why you were cut up about his jilting you.'

Taryn paused in her stirring. 'Having spent a little

35

time in Luke's company I'm beginning to realise that he's not so very much like Mark after all. Mark would never have enjoyed looking round your garden, yet Luke was really interested.'

'Would you say he compared favourably?'

The question hung in the air. It was too early in their relationship to say what she thought of Luke. She strongly resented his coming into her life and reviving all that she had tried so desperately to forget, yet there was something about him that made it impossible to dislike him altogether. He was so—she sought for the right word. Nice sounded too weak, yet she could think of no other suitable description. Gammy had obviously taken an instant liking to him, Rory too—and a child had an uncanny way of knowing whether a person was all he seemed to be on the outside. She could never imagine Luke double-crossing anyone. In fact, had he not looked like Mark she would have undoubtedly been attracted—a realisation which shook her.

'I suppose he does,' she said eventually. 'Though I wouldn't have said that in the early days. I loved him so much, Gammy, my heart felt as though it was broken in two when I found out about Maria. It's only now that I can see what a selfish man he was.'

'Yet I've no doubt you would forgive him if he asked you to take him back?'

'Would I?' Taryn's blue eyes studied her aunt for a second before she shook her head. 'I don't think so. Once bitten, twice shy.'

'I think this man's going to make a big difference in your life,' smiled Gammy. 'In fact, I would say that the rainbow's already working.'

'What do you mean?' The response was jerked from her lips.

Gammy looked at her niece candidly. 'You're so obviously right for each other.'

'How can you say that? You've only just met him.' Taryn knew that her aunt relied on her faith in the mythical powers of the rainbow and that once she'd made up her mind that it was this natural phenomenon that had brought them together nothing would persuade her otherwise.

'I know, my child, I've seen the signs. You wait and see. Time will prove me right. I hope he's not going to be too long with Rory, or dinner will be ruined.'

The subject was changed and Taryn absently carried on mixing the gravy, wondering how her aunt could be so sure.

During lunch it was Gammy and Luke who did most of the talking. Taryn remained silent, almost afraid to speak in case her aunt wrongly interpreted her words, or told Luke about the rainbow and the possible effect it could have on their lives. In fact they monopolised the conversation to such an extent that Taryn became lost in a world of her own. Sitting across the table from Luke, listening to the deep-timbred voice, watching the unusual tawny eyes alter colour with his swift changes of mood—lightening to amber when he laughed and as dark as woodland peat when he was serious—she was vividly reminded of her last dinner with Mark.

He had taken her to their favourite restaurant, treated her with the courtesy and tenderness that had been missing of late. She had been wooed into a false sense of security, almost believing that all her fears had been unfounded, that despite her apprehension he still loved her. When suddenly, without preamble, he had asked to be released from their engagement. He wanted to marry Maria! She had been shocked beyond belief. He had never told her there was any-one else. He had explained his frequent absence as business trips, cultivating new custom, arranging this show or that. To think that he had been double-crossing her all the time; it was more than she could bear.

Taryn smiled now, recalling his expression when she had stood up at the table, pushing back her chair so violently that it had fallen with a crash and brought the attention of the whole restaurant to her irate form. Tugging off her ring, she had thrown it on to the table with a force that had shattered a wine glass. 'Marry Maria!' she had spat. 'Marry whoever you like, but don't two-time her as you have me. You're despicable, Mark Vandyke, do you hear, com-pletely and utterly despicable, and I never want to see you again as long as I live!' Head held high, Taryn had stormed from the room. She had never felt so angry or humiliated in her life. She had not seen Mark since.

Unaware that a fleeting succession of emotions had crossed her face as she recollected this scene, Taryn was surprised to find her aunt and Luke watching her closely.

'Are you all right?' frowned Gammy.

'Of course,' she snapped, unable to stop the fine

edge of anger her memories had evoked.

'You look—strange,' the other woman persisted.

'I tell you there's nothing the matter.'

'Nothing?' Luke joined in her aunt's concern, looking more closely at Taryn's face. 'I should say there's a whole lot wrong with you. Perhaps it's the heat in here. Shall I open the door?'

'For God's sake!' Taryn pushed away her unfinished food and planted her hands firmly on the table. 'If you're really so interested I'll tell you.' She ignored her aunt and glared at the man seated opposite. 'Every time I see you I'm reminded of Mark. It's bad enough at a distance, but how do you think I feel now—sitting so close I have only to reach out my hand to touch you? Looking at a face which is so hauntingly like the man I loved that it's enough to drive me out of my mind. Why have you come here? Why are you doing this to me?' Then she covered her face with her hands and rushed from the room.

Luke made to follow, but Gammy put a restraining hand on his arm. 'Best leave her alone. It's been a great shock, but she'll get over it. She'll soon get used to you.'

Taryn heard her aunt's counsel as she mounted the stairs. How easy it was to convince yourself with a few well chosen words. But she would never be able to look at Luke without being reminded of Mark. She ought not to have taken the job. It would never work out.

Lying on the bed, Taryn stared at the sloping ceiling, finally deciding that she must tell Luke she could not work for him. Painful memories that had taken so long to erase were all too easily revived. She would never be able to face Luke without recalling this last final scene which had been her degradation. It was no use fooling herself any longer that the wounds had healed, and working with Luke would only open them further.

Determinedly she sprang to her feet and after running a brush through her hair made her faltering way back down to the living room. On the bottom stair she halted. Gammy sat alone, the remains of their meal still on the table.

'Where's Luke?' Taryn's voice was a mere whisper.

'Gone. He couldn't wait for you to come out of your tantrum.'

'I was not in a tantrum,' retorted Taryn, 'I was merely telling him the truth.'

Gammy snorted. 'You sounded very rude to me. I don't know what's come over you. I've never known you behave like this before. Have you forgotten that you're going to work for him?'

But Taryn was not listening. She was across the room and out of the door, running down the path to the road. Perhaps she could stop him; perhaps it wasn't too late—but there was no one in sight and as she looked towards the top field the helicopter rose into the air. He flew low across the valley. Taryn waved frantically, and he saw her. So close was the aircraft that she saw the white of his teeth as he smiled. She shouted to him to come back, but her words were borne away on the wind. His hand waved in salute before he lifted with sudden swiftness and disappeared into the blue summer sky.

In chagrin Taryn bit her lip. He thought she was saying goodbye. She turned, startled to find Gammy at her side.

'He left a message,' remarked the older woman. 'He said you're to go up to Dale End tomorrow and explain to his man exactly what you want doing.'

'But, Gammy,' Taryn's face crumpled, 'I've changed my mind. I wanted to tell him—it won't work out. You saw my reaction. I can't do it.' The last words were choked from her lips, and placing an arm about her niece's shoulders Gammy led her back into the cottage.

'You're overwrought,' she consoled. 'It's been a shock. You'll adjust in time.'

Taryn shook her head. 'Never. To me he will always be Mark—and I hate him!' Her voice rose hysterically. 'Oh, Gammy, it's against the laws of nature for two men to look so alike. Do you still think he can really be Mark?'

'I don't know what to think, love. All I know is that he seems a nice enough man, whoever he is, and if you know what's good for you you'll start that job tomorrow and act as though he's any normal employer. Work is what you need right now, and by the time Luke's back you'll have grown used to the idea of seeing him about.'

'I suppose you're right,' admitted Taryn. 'Do you know when he'll be coming?'

'He said something about the weekend. That's four days to pull yourself together.'

Taryn went early to the house the next day. Her aunt

was right. She did need something to occupy her mind. Every waking hour, every minute, every second, her thoughts dwelled constantly on Luke. She had lain awake far into the night, unable to banish from her mind this man who had ravaged her calm, entered into her valley of peace, crushed with one mighty blow the fence she had built round her broken heart. Did Luke himself know the anguish he had caused? Could he guess how it felt to be so reminded of the man who had tossed her casually to one side? Her thoughts ran on and on in the same vein until she felt bemused and unable to face the new day. Only Gammy's plain speaking had brought her to her senses.

'There's no point in brooding, love. Whatever will be will be, as the song goes, and very true it is. Luke can't help what he looks like, and it's up to you to accept him as he is and forget all about everything else. You've let that Italian affair upset you too much, though I've never told you so before. Now you've got an interesting job you must count it as a blessing. Everything happens for the best, even if it doesn't look like it at the time.'

Taryn recalled her aunt's words as she climbed up to Dale End and smiled wryly. Gammy was rarely wrong. A Land Rover was parked at the side of the house, its tracks clearly outlined in the overgrown drive—the only vehicle to use the path for many years.

The heavy front door stood open. Taryn walked inside, her shoes making a staccato of sound on the bare boards. She thought now, as she had on her first visit, how strange it was that the house should be completely bare. She had somehow expected everything to be as it was when the old man died, but instead it had been divested of carpets, curtains, furniture, the lot. Not so much as a box remained to give an indication of its previous owner. It made their job easier, without a doubt, yet it gave the house a curiously detached air. Again she gave an involuntary shiver and looked over her shoulder as if expecting to see old Henry's ghost. When someone spoke she cried out in surprise.

'There's no need to be nervous, lass. Didn't you know I was here?'

As the owner of the gruff voice moved into the shaft of sunlight that filtered in through the open door Taryn breathed in relief. This was no spirit—a tall, broad man in his early fifties, skin weathered to a rich mahogany and twinkling blue eyes that watched her with amusement.

She nodded. 'I guessed you were, but it's this house, it gives me the creeps.'

'There's nothing here to be afeared of,' he said. 'I guess you must be Miss Penreath? The gaffer told me you'd be coming. Andrew Shire's the name, but I'd be pleased if you'd call me Andy.' He extended a brown, work-worn hand.

'And I'm Taryn,' she responded. 'Has Luke—Mr Major—left any instructions? He showed me around yesterday, but apart from telling me which room he wanted for his study he said no more.'

'I've a plan here.' Andy pulled a piece of paper from his pocket. 'The gaffer has made one or two

43

suggestions, but he says you're in charge of the whole operation.'

Taryn was amazed that Luke should give her so much responsibility. What did she know of his likes and dislikes, his tastes, his preferences? And how did he know he could rely on her? He knew she hadn't done this type of work before. He really was a most trusting man.

'See here,' Andy stabbed at the paper with a grimy forefinger, indicating the south-western tower room, 'This is to be the day lounge, because it gets the benefit of the sun for most of the day, and next to it——'

But Taryn was no longer listening. Her eyes had travelled across the page to the elevation of the first floor, and the room immediately above the day lounge. There was nothing extraordinary in what she saw, so why the sudden tightening in her throat?

Andy followed her gaze. 'Yes,' he said, 'that's Mrs Major's room; he was most emphatic about that. Said it must be the best one. Mr Major's next to it, here, and he wants an adjoining door putting in and a bathroom opposite. Everything else he said I could leave to you.'

'I see.' So Luke was married. Somehow she had imagined him to be single—like Mark—or as Mark had been, she quickly corrected herself. He too would be a married man by this time. She felt vaguely disappointed by her discovery, yet was at a loss to understand why, and something else puzzled her too—why separate rooms? Did he not share his wife's bed? Was there disharmony between them? These were questions she could not answer. Another thought suddenly struck her. 'Has Luke any children?'

'Why, no, lass,' replied Andy. 'What must you be thinking of?'

She felt even more disturbed by the strange look he gave her. 'I just wondered,' she said, 'that's all. If you're ready we'll make a start.' She looked about her at the dingy walls covered in faded brown paper, falling from the corners as if pleading to be removed. The doors too were dark brown, flaking and dirty. It was a large, lofty hall, with stairs leading up from either side of a central fireplace. 'I want this doing in light pastel shades,' she said. 'I think perhaps pale gold walls to represent sunlight, with ivory paintwork. We'll have a huge mirror on the wall above the fireplace to reflect the light from the window—and a crystal chandelier.' She looked down at the floor. 'It's a shame to cover these boards. We'll have them polished until you can see your face in them, with a Persian carpet in the middle. And plenty of flowers,' she continued, 'I'll do those myself. Oh, I can just imagine it!'

Andy was watching her with admiration. 'I can see why the gaffer said to leave everything to you. You certainly know what will suit the old place best.'

Taryn's enthusiasm was building up. Already she was forgetting her antagonism towards Luke. She wished he was here to discuss her plans, to guide her when she hesitated, perhaps argue over her choice. And then there was the question of money. How much did he wish her to spend? Had she a free hand in ordering the furniture and carpets? It would cost a small fortune to create a home out of this empty shell of a house.

She smiled at Andy. 'It's easy when you're spending someone else's money. Is Mr Major very wealthy?'

'He's better off than most,' he replied, 'though not as rich as some,' which answer told her precisely nothing.

She tried again. 'I believe he has his own business. Do you know what it is?'

'Oh, yes,' he nodded. 'He owns a chain of hotels. Hence the "chopper" for getting from one to the other quickly.'

Horror crossed her face. 'He's not thinking of turning this place into a——'

Andy shook his head. 'You need have no fears there. This is going to be his retreat. He has a flat in London and one in Edinburgh, but between you and me I think he's feeling the strain and needs some quiet little backwater where he can forget all his worries.'

Taryn smiled. 'I wouldn't call this small, but it's certainly quiet. How did he find it?'

'He pored over lists and lists before he came across this one,' he said. 'He made up his mind on the spot— and I can't say I blame him; it's an ideal position to get away from the hustle and bustle of town life.'

As Andy appeared to be in an expansive mood, Taryn asked next, 'Has Luke ever been to Italy?'

'I expect so,' confirmed the man. 'He's been nearly all over the world.'

'I mean, has he ever spent any length of time there?'

Andy shrugged. 'He could have done. He does sometimes disappear abroad for a month or two, but he doesn't confide in me. Why do you ask?'

'I once saw someone who looked like him.' Taryn tried to keep her voice casual, not wishing him to know the effect Luke Major had on her.

'Ah—it's said everyone has a double, though I suppose it's possible you could have seen the gaffer. Have you asked him?'

Taryn shook her head. 'Not yet.'

'Then I should. He'll soon tell you if it was him.'

They moved then to the next room and in the excitement of creating beauty out of the grime and squalor of Dale End Taryn forgot for a while her disquieted thoughts. She even forgot about lunch, and it was after five before she returned to her aunt's cottage, tired, hungry, more than a little dirty, yet for the first time in months genuinely happy.

Gammy took one look at the girl's face and smiled, a quietly satisfied smile, though wisely she said nothing. 'I've run your bath,' she said. 'I saw you coming. Go and have a nice long soak while I get your tea.'

It was much later in the evening before Taryn told her aunt that Luke was married.

Gammy's head shot up and she looked at Taryn sharply. 'Are you sure? He said nothing to me, and we had quite a long chat the other day.'

'Positive. Andy showed me a plan of the house. Luke had marked on it exactly which room he wanted for his wife.'

Great-aunt Margaret passed a hand across her brow. 'I can't believe it. There must be some mistake.'

Taryn was forced to smile. 'You mean you don't want to believe it. You're cherishing the idea that Luke and I will get together one day. Sorry to disappoint you, dear aunt, but that's the way it goes.'

CHAPTER THREE

Two cars drew up outside Honeysuckle Cottage the next morning. This was such an uncommon occurrence that both Taryn and her aunt rushed outside to see what was happening.

'Miss Penreath?' One of the drivers got out and looked questioningly at the two women.

'I'm Miss Penreath,' replied Taryn.

'The car you hired,' he said smartly. 'You should find it satisfactory.'

'But I didn't—I haven't hired a car.'

He pulled a slip of paper from his pocket. 'Miss Penreath, Honeysuckle Cottage, Ferndale. One car for an unlimited period—it's all here. Good day, ma'am.'

Taryn stared as he climbed into the other car. 'Er— thank you,' she called lamely after them as they disappeared in a cloud of dust. 'What do you make of this?' she asked, turning to her aunt.

'Beats me,' shrugged the other woman.

At that moment a motor-cycle came over the brow of the hill and squealed to a halt beside them. 'Telegram for Miss Penreath.'

Taryn's eyebrows slid up in astonishment. What on earth was going on? She tore open the envelope and read, TRUST CAR HAS ARRIVED. FORGOT YOU WILL NEED SOMETHING TO GET ABOUT WHEN ORDERING THE FURNITURE, ETC. HOPE ALL IS GOING WELL. REGARDS,

Wordlessly she passed it to Gammy, who smiled, 'How thoughtful,' and to the boy who stood waiting, 'There's no reply.'

'How did he know I could drive?' asked Taryn.

'I should imagine that in his world all women drive and naturally he assumed you did too. This gesture makes me like him even more.'

'You liked him right from the beginning, didn't you, Gammy? At least it's solved my question as to whether he was leaving me to order the furnishings,' and, suddenly excited, 'Shall we go into Exeter to-day? There used to be a marvellous antique shop that has just the sort of thing I'm looking for.'

'I'm sorry.' Gammy looked disappointed. 'I've promised to bake some cakes for the school fête. Take Janice, she'll enjoy the change. She was only moaning the other day that she never gets out nowadays. Once the baby's born she'll have plenty to do, it's the waiting that gets her down.'

Taryn laughed. 'You too. You can't wait to be a great-grandmother, but it's a good idea all the same. I'll go and ask her.'

Janice was of the same age as Taryn. They had been to school together, shared each other's secrets, and until Taryn's disastrous affair had kept nothing back. But since returning to the valley Taryn had felt disinclined to talk and had not seen so much of Janice. Newly married herself, her cousin had been too en-grossed with her new husband to seek out Taryn, but it would be nice to spend a few hours with her again.

As Gammy had foretold, Janice was delighted at the prospect of a day spent shopping and before long they were on their way.

'What's he like, this new boss of yours?' Janice asked, trying to settle her unaccustomed bulk into the limited space of the car. Her pregnancy suited her. Once a thin pale girl, she now looked the picture of health. Her skin glowed and her eyes sparkled and her short dark hair was in tip-top condition. Not as tall as Taryn, she was now pleasantly rounded, but instead of bewailing the loss of her figure she was contented and happy and looked forward to the day when she became a mother.

Taryn realised there was no point in avoiding the issue. 'I expect you've heard by now that he looks like Mark? Honestly, Janice, it's the most weird thing that's ever happened to me.'

'I think it's exciting. Everyone's talking about it.'

'I might have known,' replied Taryn. 'I've been too busy to become involved myself, but I guessed it wouldn't be long before they all knew.'

'Well, come on then, what's he like, this hero of yours?'

Taryn threw her cousin a disdainful look. 'Very kind, very charming and very handsome. But I don't like him.'

'Why on earth not?' queried Janice, wide-eyed.

'For the very reason I gave earlier—because he reminds me of Mark.' She kept her eyes on the road ahead, shimmering in the heat of the day.

'I don't understand you, Taryn. Just because one

man jilted you there's no reason to dislike another. Give him a chance.'

Taryn sniffed. 'You're as bad as Gammy! If either of you had met Mark you'd appreciate the way I feel.'

'How about this rumour I've heard that he could be suffering from loss of memory?' persisted Janice.

'Another of Gammy's theories. You know what she's like. If you believe everything you hear you're a fool. The truth of the matter is Gammy's trying to make this rubbish about the rainbow come true.'

'You mean you actually saw *the* rainbow—the one we always looked for when we were children? And then you met Mr Major?' Janice sounded awed. 'No wonder Gammy's——'

'Don't say you believe it too,' scoffed Taryn. 'For Pete's sake, have a bit of sense.'

'We believed it when we were young,' protested Janice, 'so why not now? After all, both our parents saw it *and* met their husbands shortly afterwards.'

'But *you* didn't, and no one's going to make me believe that Luke's the man for me. He's my boss—full stop. Besides which,' she paused to get the full effect from her words, 'he's already married.'

Janice's reaction was much the same as Gammy's. Her mouth fell open and she stared at Taryn. 'No! That's one piece of news that's escaped the village grapevine.' And then on a more sympathetic note, 'Poor you. So there'll be no chance of——'

'There never was,' interrupted Taryn firmly.

Janice grimaced. 'What's she like, this wife of Luke's?'

'No idea. It would be better if I had, then I would

know what sort of furniture to choose for *her* bedroom.'

Janice's brows rose. 'They have separate rooms?' and as Taryn nodded, 'How strange—even so, if I were moving into a new house I would want to supervise the furnishing of my own room at least.'

'Me too, but that's the way it is, so I shall just have to do the best I can.'

Taryn drove on in silence for the next few miles, temporarily regretting living in such a close-knit community. Nothing was sacred, no business too private not to be shared with the neighbours. But as they neared Exeter her spirits rose. It should be fun seeking out the appropriate furniture to suit Dale End.

The antique shop was still there; overflowing with chairs and tables, pictures and lamps, brass, copper, china and glass. Taryn was soon lost in a world of her own, only occasionally remembering Janice and throwing her the odd remark. 'Look at this blue and gilt china clock—oh, I must have that, and this French mirror—it's just what I need for the hall. Oh, and look at that Boulle table—isn't it beautiful?'

It was lunch time before she finished browsing. Janice sat in a cane chair near the door, completely exhausted. 'I'm sorry,' exclaimed Taryn, suddenly noticing her cousin's pale face. 'I'd forgotten you tire easily these days. Shall we have lunch, and then if you feel up to it I'd like to look in that new shop that's opened round the corner. There's a super four-poster bed in the window which would be perfect for Mrs Major's room.'

'You're taking a gamble there. What if she doesn't

like it? Why don't you ask Mr Major what he thinks?'

'Mm, I suppose I could, but it is my job, so if she disapproves of my choice that's her bad luck.'

'You sound as though you don't like her very much. It's not like you to talk like that about anyone.'

Taryn smiled ruefully, but not for anything would she admit that the thought of Luke's wife was disturbing. This was a feeling even she herself could not understand.

When they arrived back at Ferndale Taryn was surprised to see a white Volvo outside her aunt's cottage. Visitors were rare in this secluded village and she wondered who it could be. She dropped off an inquisitive Janice and pulled up behind the expensive-looking car.

She ought to have known. Who else would arrive in such style? Immediately she opened the door the deep tones of his voice reached her ears. 'Ah, Taryn. I hoped you wouldn't be long.'

He was alone in the room. 'Hello, Luke. This is a surprise. Gammy said you weren't coming until the weekend. Where is she?'

'Making tea—as usual. This is only a flying visit, I'm afraid. I was in Bristol, so thought I'd call in and see how things were going.'

'But that's miles away,' exclaimed Taryn.

'Not the way I drive.'

'That reminds me, thank you for hiring the Mini. You really shouldn't have bothered.'

'And how would you have got about?' he scoffed. 'I can't imagine Dainty taking kindly to the towns.'

'I'd have managed,' she said, 'but I must admit it's a big help. Have you been here long?'

'A few minutes—but I can't stay. You've met Andy?'

'Oh, yes. We had a good session yesterday.' Her eyes lit up. 'I'm really looking forward to the transformation of Dale End. I've started ordering the furniture already. By the way, do you think Mrs Major would like a four-poster bed? I've seen a gorgeous one in Exeter which would fit into the tower room perfectly.'

He smiled at her enthusiasm. 'I'm sure she would. I don't think you need worry about her not liking anything you choose. She's very adaptable.'

What a peculiar way of describing his wife, mused Taryn, before continuing, 'One other thing, is there any limit on money? I'm having everything charged to you at Dale End.'

'Spend what you like,' he said agreeably. 'I can afford it.'

How nice not to have to count the cost, thought Taryn drily. Mark had been the same; money had meant nothing to him—easily gained and easily lost.

'Now what are you thinking?' he asked. 'You really must learn to guard your feelings, Taryn. You were looking at me then as though you positively loathed me.'

'I was?' Taryn sounded surprised. 'I didn't mean to.'

'It was Mark again, wasn't it? Aren't you ever going to stop relating the two of us?'

Taryn sighed. 'If only I could! You can't imagine

55

how difficult it is.'

'Indeed I can, but I think it's a matter of being strong-minded. You're not trying hard enough. Every time you look at me you think of the other man, whether consciously or not I don't know. Take the other day——'

'Yes,' cut in Taryn, 'I must apologise for my behaviour. I'm sorry, I'll try not to let it happen again.'

'Your aunt says you almost changed your mind about the job?'

'I *did* change my mind. If you hadn't gone I should have told you. I can't help how I feel, Luke. I do try, believe me, but Mark has scarred me for life whether I like it or not.'

'He sounds a bit of a cad. I hope you don't really compare me with him?'

Taryn smiled. 'Not character-wise. I'm beginning to find that out. It would be interesting to see you both together. Have you been to Italy?'

His thick brows rose. 'Is that where you met him?' and as Taryn nodded, 'I was there last year, as a matter of fact. In Naples. I was——'

He stopped and Taryn urged him on, her heart beating a sudden tattoo within her breast. 'You were what?'

'I thought of opening a hotel there,' he said casually, 'but I changed my mind. Ah, here's tea, and then I must go.'

Was this sufficient proof of his identity? Taryn still was not sure. As he drank his tea and chatted to Gammy she studied him even more closely, trying to find some difference in his appearance that would confirm once and for all that he was not Mark. His thick, dark hair swept across his brow at exactly the same angle, fine lines were etched at the corners of his eyes, his cheeks dimpled when he smiled. It was impossible to find any distinguishing mark. She shook her head. The more she pondered the more bewildering the whole affair became.

He left shortly afterwards, and judging by her aunt's face she was highly satisfied by his visit. Not wishing to talk about him now, Taryn decided to go up to Dale End and see how the work was progressing.

Gammy expressed surprise. 'I don't think Luke would want you to put in so much time,' she said. 'You've been out all day.'

'That was pleasure,' remarked Taryn. 'I enjoyed it tremendously. Anyway, I'll only be about an hour.'

Already she was beginning to wear a path up the slope and the journey was much easier than on that first day. The westering sun depicted the house in sharp relief against a golden haze of sky. It still looked gaunt and forbidding, but Taryn was no longer apprehensive. She was beginning to love this old building and looked forward to the day when its conversion was complete.

She paused to rest for a moment on an old lichen-covered bench in the garden. Closing her eyes, she listened to the warbling of a thrush, the raucous cry of a rook and the more homely chirping of the sparrows. Up here on the hill, in splendid isolation, an all-pervading peace stole over her. She could almost forget her troubles. Luke had certainly made a wise choice.

She suddenly realised it was too quiet. Surely there should be sounds of activity from within the house? She ran to the front door, but it resisted her touch. Then she looked at her watch. Of course, work would be finished for the day; what a fool she was—and she had no key.

Perhaps Andy had left a window open? She wandered round the house, without success. The back door too was securely fastened. Then she saw it, a tiny window open—high in the wall. It probably belonged to the pantry, but it looked just big enough for her to wriggle through.

It was stupid to want to climb into Dale End, she knew, but now she was here she did not want to go back without seeing what work had been done; but first of all she must find something to stand on.

A search of the nearby outhouses revealed a water butt almost hidden by creeping ivy. It was empty apart from the myriads of insects who had made it their home. It was heavy too, but she managed to drag it across the cobbled yard and turn it upside down beneath the window. From then on it was a simple matter to climb up and ease herself through the window. Or so she thought. Her head and one shoulder went through, but the opening was smaller than she had anticipated. Still determined to get inside, she wriggled and struggled, tearing the thin material of her blouse in the process, but eventually both shoulders were through.

Suddenly her ankles were held in a vice-like grip.

'Caught you, my lad! What do you think you're playing at?'

Luke! His voice was unmistakable. And he thought she was a boy trying to break into the house! It was easy to understand why when he could only see her faded blue jeans.

'It—it's me,' she faltered.

Silence.

Then, '*Taryn!* What the blazes are you doing?'

'I—I——' She tried to twist round to look at him, but in her undignified position found it impossible. 'I wanted to see how the work was going.'

'Didn't you think of using the door?' his voice heavy with sarcasm.

'I have no key.'

'So—you thought it important enough to break in. I don't expect you to work night and day, but if you still insist on having a look we'll use the proper entrance. Come on down.'

He sounded dreadfully annoyed and Taryn took a deep breath before saying, 'I—I can't. I had an awful job getting through this far. And—and, Luke, there's nothing to hold on to. I can't get down this way either.' She had been wrong in assuming it was the pantry. The window was high in the wall of a passage with a drop of about nine feet.

She heard his snort of impatience. 'Trust a woman! Hold on, I'll come and help from inside.'

In the few minutes before he reached her Taryn realised what a ridiculous position she had got herself into. She could get neither in nor out. She hated to think what would have happened had Luke not turned up. Perhaps she would have eventually managed to get down the other side, but even so she would never have got out again. It would have meant spending the night in the house. The haunted house! A prickle of fear ran down her spine. It was easy to convince herself she didn't believe in old Henry's ghost in the sane light of day, but in the still of the night—she would be scared half out of her wits.

Luke appeared now, a tall, shadowy figure in the gloom of the house. He carried a pair of step ladders. 'Hurrah for Andy,' he said drily, putting them down beneath Taryn's protruding body. In two seconds he was pulling her the rest of the way through the window frame. Her feet found the steps, and then she was down. Reaction set in and her legs felt so weak that she unconsciously clung to Luke for support. She made no demur when his arms tightened about her shoulders. 'You silly little goose,' he murmured. 'I thought you had more sense.'

She looked up, saw the tender smile on his face and stiffened. How many times had Mark looked at her in just that way? She shook her head and struggled to free herself. She must get away. This was madness.

Luke released her the instant he saw her reaction. 'Don't worry,' he said, misinterpreting her reason, 'I won't molest you, though if anyone saw us now I'd have a hard job convincing them otherwise.'

He looked at the front of her blouse. Taryn had forgotten it was torn and to her humiliation saw that it revealed most of her very brief underwear. Colour flooded her cheeks. Desperately she clutched together with one hand the remainder of her shirt. 'Don't flatter yourself,' she said tightly, 'that thought was farthest from my mind.'

'Then what—oh, lord, don't say we're back to that again? Listen here, young Taryn, it's about time we had a serious talk about Mark Vandyke.'

'Don't young Taryn me,' she retorted hotly.

'Is twenty so old?' he mocked. 'As I can give you all of thirteen years you seem very young to me. Of course, I could be mistaken, but I would have thought that a *mature* twenty-year-old would consider it beneath her dignity to scramble through windows.'

Taryn turned her back on him and took refuge in silence. There was nothing she could say. He was determined to get the upper hand.

'Shall we talk outside?' he asked pleasantly, almost as though nothing had happened. 'It's quite cool in here.'

'If you like.' Taryn followed him along the corridor, resentful of his apparent indifference.

Once outside he carefully locked the door and handed her the key. 'Andy should have given you one, but you'd better have this in case you decide to make any more evening calls.'

'I doubt it,' came her brief reply as she walked with him to his car.

'Now,' he said, after they were settled, 'suppose you tell me all about your ill-fated love affair? Once you get it out of your system perhaps our relationship will stand a better chance.'

'As I'm only your employee,' said Taryn, studying a tiny fly as it walked across the windscreen, 'I can't see that it really matters.'

'But it does,' he insisted. 'How can you expect to put your best into your work when you resent me?'

She looked at him then. 'It's not you personally. It's——'

'I know—but it amounts to the same thing.' His voice deepened. 'Wouldn't you like to tell me?'

'If you insist—though I don't think it will help.'

'Let me be the judge of that.' He touched her hand briefly. 'Start when you're ready.'

It took a full two minutes for Taryn to summon up the courage to talk about Mark. She had once vowed to herself never to bring up the past again. It still had the power to hurt.

'It all began when I went to work as a fabric designer for Vandyke Fashions in Naples. It was my first job after leaving college and I didn't care that it was in a strange country or that I wouldn't know anyone. It was the culmination of all my dreams. I was so excited that it was only after a few weeks I realised the job was not all I had imagined it to be. I worked long hours and I was treated as a junior most of the time, which I suppose is what I was, although I was too full of my own importance to realise it.'

Luke smiled as though agreeing, but he said nothing and waited for her to continue.

'One night when I'd been working later than usual I felt so sorry for myself that I began to cry. I couldn't help it, and once I'd started I couldn't stop. Then I became aware of someone watching me, and through my tears I saw Mark Vandyke. I was so ashamed. It was the first time I'd met the great man himself, and that he should see me like that—I blabbered an apology, expecting him to demand to know what was going on. Instead he passed me a handkerchief and came down on his knees beside me. The next thing I knew I was telling him how lonely I was and he had invited me out to dinner.' She paused, pulling the corners of her lips down wryly as she recalled the occasion. 'That was the first of many invitations. Things snowballed quickly from there. I was no longer a nobody, I was the envy of everyone, and a few weeks later we were engaged.'

'Quite an achievement,' remarked Luke. 'So what happened to spoil your rhapsody?'

'He began to make excuses not to see me, and innocent fool that I was, I believed him, though I must admit that sometimes when he said he was meeting a buyer or someone like that I wondered why he couldn't take me along too. My job was quite important by then. My work was gaining recognition and I was earning a name in my own right. When once or twice my friends—I had some by then—tried to warn me what was happening I wouldn't listen. Mark would never two-time me, I thought. He loves me. I would look at my ring and imagine a gold band at its side. I was quite sure that one day we would be married.' Her voice broke. 'I shall never forget the day he told me about Maria. He asked me to release him from our engagement. I couldn't believe him at first, and then I was so angry. I've never been so mad in my whole life. Goodness knows what I called him—but I vowed that I'd never speak to him again as long as I live. I'd rather die first.'

Luke was silent for a few moments. 'Thank you,'

he said at last. 'I think I understand a little more clearly now why you feel as you do about me. I've no idea why we should look alike, but I can assure you that I am not Mark.' He paused and leaned closer towards her, his eyes searching her face. 'You're still not convinced? There's one way we could find out.' His shoulder brushed hers. She could feel his breath warm against her cheek.

She began to tremble and closed her eyes to try and shut out the vision. He was Mark. He must be. He'd got to be!

Luke took her action as a sign of assent. Suddenly his lips were on hers, tenderly, experimentally— with none of the passion she had experienced under Mark's embraces. Luke was feeling his way, afraid to hurry, yet anxious for her reaction. For one long second she remained submissive beneath his touch, even though every fibre of her being called out in response, then with a shuddering sigh she pushed him away. 'How dare you!' she snapped, more angry with herself than with Luke, but determined not to let him know this. 'How dare you take advantage!'

He was unperturbed. 'I'm only trying to prove something.' His eyes were as light as amber and the dimples hovered in his cheeks as he suppressed a smile. 'How did I compare?'

Taryn glared. 'Abysmally. I guess you're right— Mark never kissed me like that.'

'Ah, but you didn't give me a fair trial. I'd hardly got going. Maybe we'd better make sure.' He edged forward.

Taryn pressed back against the door, her breast

heaving beneath the tight shirt which she still clutched with one hand. 'You touch me again and I'll——'

He quirked a brow and waited.

'I'll never forgive you,' she finished bravely.

'You're very fond of making dramatic statements,' he chuckled. 'I wonder if you ever carry them out. I've a good mind to try and—where are you going?' as the door swung open beneath her touch.

'Home,' she retorted. 'I don't want to sit here and listen to you any longer.'

He looked at her shirt. 'Like that? What *will* the neighbours think? Come on, I'll take you.'

Ungraciously Taryn slammed the door. He was right—she daren't walk through the village like this. Lips pressed together, she stared straight ahead and waited for him to start.

'I wish I understood you,' he said, as the car turned an arc in the drive. 'I really am only trying to help.'

'I'll find my own solution, thanks,' she asserted quietly, 'and if you don't mind my saying so I think the less I see of you the better. You can pass on your instructions through Andy.' Immediately the words were out she regretted them. This wasn't how one spoke to an employer. It would serve her right if he sacked her on the spot.

'Suit yourself,' he said lightly, though had she looked across she would have seen the tightening of his jaw. 'So long as the work is carried out to my satisfaction I can't see that it matters one way or the other. And if it will help you——' He left the sentence in mid-air.

There was silence between them for the rest of the short journey. Outside the cottage Taryn murmured a quick, 'Thank you for the lift,' and fled indoors before he could speak.

Great-aunt Margaret looked up in surprise as her niece dashed through the living room, her blouse flying open and the suspicion of tears on her face. And when she heard Luke's car pull away she was even more astounded, but shrewdly she allowed Taryn to proceed upstairs unchecked, knowing that in time she would learn what was troubling the girl.

As for Taryn herself, she lay on the bed and allowed her tears to flow freely. She was shaken and afraid—afraid of her own response to Luke's kisses. Why, oh, why had he set her pulse racing? What had caused this reaction? Was it Luke himself who evoked these feelings, or his resemblance to Mark? She arrived at no tangible answer, knowing only that she must keep a tighter rein on her emotions. It would never do to become involved a second time—whether with the same man or someone else.

Half an hour passed before she felt calmer. Smiling ruefully to herself, she changed into a clean shirt, splashed cold water on to her face and went downstairs to face Gammy.

A pot of tea stood on the table—her aunt's remedy for all occasions. Gammy sat knitting and pretending to concentrate on the intricate pattern as Taryn poured herself a drink. Taryn knew it was a front; her aunt was full of curiosity but was too polite to question her.

'Well, go on,' Taryn encouraged, 'why don't you

ask me what happened? I can see you're dying to know.'

Gammy nodded. 'Naturally, but I also know you will tell me when you're ready.'

'Well, it would be nice if you showed a bit of enthusiasm instead of sitting there as though I'd just come back from the pictures or something. What do you think happened? Didn't you see my blouse?' Sometimes Gammy's calm manner irritated her, and today was one of those occasions.

The old lady's eyes twinkled. 'I saw—and I know what construction most people would put on it—but I'm not most people and I know my own niece well enough to realise that she wouldn't get up to any hanky-panky.'

'I can't get you going, can I?' grumbled Taryn goodnaturedly. She felt nearer to her own normal self now and could laugh at the situation which less than an hour ago had driven her almost to distraction.

She proceeded to tell her aunt about the predicament in which she had landed herself and their discussion about Mark, followed by Luke's suggestion that he should try and prove his identity by kissing her.

This amused her aunt tremendously. 'So typical of the impression I've gained,' she said, 'but did it help?'

'Who can say?' Taryn deliberately kept her tone casual. 'It would be wrong to try and compare. The circumstances weren't right.'

'Then you're not as indifferent as you make out?'

'I don't know what you mean.'

'If his attentions hadn't affected you, I hardly

think you'd have come flying in here as though all hell had let loose. You can't escape love.'

'*Love!*' Taryn flashed scornfully. 'It will be a long time before I fall in love again—if ever—and it certainly won't be with Luke Major. Besides which,' she added as an afterthought, 'aren't you forgetting he's married?'

'No, no, but I'd rather not dwell on that aspect at the moment.'

'When we're talking about love I should think it's of paramount importance. Anyway, I've told him it will be best if we steer clear of each other in future.'

Gammy looked up sharply. 'You surprise me sometimes, Taryn. Don't you think you're behaving childishly?'

'Maybe,' she shrugged, 'but I can't help it. You don't know what it's like being confronted with—with—oh, you know what I mean.' She crashed her cup down into its saucer and moved towards the door. 'I think I'll go out on Dainty for an hour; try and refresh myself.'

Out on the moors she let the horse have his head. For three days he had been neglected and now behaved like a child out of school, racing, prancing, leaping. Taryn laughed aloud and dug in her heels. 'Come on, boy, come on!'

With her hair streaming out behind and the wind whistling in her ears she felt a sudden release from the tensions of the last few hours. Nothing touched her here—on top of the world. She felt as light as thistledown, as free as the wind. Her troubles were forgotten.

Mile after mile they covered until at last Dainty grew tired and stopped. Taryn slipped from the saddle, and he whinnied and nuzzled her affectionately. 'You needed that, didn't you, beauty? And so did I. I feel better already.'

The fiery sun slipped slowly below the horizon. Pink feather-light clouds drifted lazily across the darkening sky. If only she could always feel like this; if only she had never met Mark—or Luke.

But she had, and Gammy was right; running away would solve nothing. She must show Luke that he meant nothing to her; that his resemblance to Mark made no difference. Surely she was grown up enough to control her feelings? All she had to do was treat her employer as just that. Forget the past and try to carry out this job to the best of her ability.

It was with renewed determination that she mounted Dainty a short while later and turned his nose for home. All would be well now. She knew exactly what she must do.

CHAPTER FOUR

THURSDAY and Friday came and went without any more visits from Luke. Taryn spent her time between Dale End and searching the local antique shops for the right furniture to blend in with the picture she was trying to create. It was such a gracious house it would be a pity to ruin it by introducing modern stuff. She was not so worried about the period as she knew that carefully chosen pieces, even though of different eras, would ultimately fuse into a harmonious whole.

She loved the work and woke each day eagerly anticipating the hours ahead. It was not until the third morning when she saw the birdlike craft in the top field that she realised today was Saturday and that her employer had arrived for the weekend. Some of her happiness disappeared and her heart fluttered apprehensively. She had intended going up to the house, but now decided against it. After all, she argued with herself, she was entitled to some spare time, though up till now she had not cared what hours she worked. The joy of bringing beauty to the long-neglected building had meant more to her than sticking to a strict time schedule. I'll take Rory into Seacombe, she decided impetuously, he'll enjoy a day by the sea.

Her mind made up, she told Gammy where she was going and hurried along to her brother's house. As she had expected, Rory was delighted at the prospect of a day out with his adorable Aunt Taryn. She was young enough to be good company yet old enough to accept responsibility for his safety.

Taryn felt no qualms about using the blue Mini for her day out and Rory himself was full of excitement. They spent many hours walking and exploring, swimming and sunbathing, and it was late in the evening before they finally returned to Ferndale Valley.

She deposited her tired but happy nephew at his parents' home before pulling up outside Honeysuckle Cottage. The light was on in the tiny front room and the curtains drawn, which should have told Taryn something, for her aunt never closed the curtains until she was home, but unsuspectingly she pushed open the door. Immediately she heard his voice a pang of disappointment struck her that he had not kept his word. Luke had given every impression of being a very honourable person who would not go back on his promise, yet here he was drinking her aunt's home-brewed elderberry wine and obviously waiting her return. Although she had vowed to let him upset her no more she could not help feeling disturbed. She swallowed the sudden lump in her throat. 'Hello, Luke.'

His smile embraced her and as if reading her thoughts he said, 'I apologise for breaking our agreement. I saw you go this morning and thought I'd pay your aunt my respects. I didn't intend staying this long, but I'm afraid I was bullied into it.'

Gammy smiled graciously. 'I couldn't let you return to those miserable lodgings and I know you want to stay near your house.'

'I'm more than grateful, dear lady,' and turning back to Taryn, 'What sort of day have you had?'

But Taryn did not hear. She was staring at Gammy. Did she mean that—no, it was impossible. She couldn't have asked Luke to stay *here*. She knew how Taryn felt. Besides, where would he sleep? They only had two bedrooms.

'Taryn.' Luke spoke again. 'You look very strange. Sure you haven't been overdoing the sunbathing?'

She looked at him then. 'Quite sure. I'm tired, though. I think I'll go to bed if you'll excuse me.'

Luke looked swiftly at her aunt and Taryn knew that her fears were justified.

'Taryn dear, come and help me make some tea, there's something I must tell you.'

Obediently Taryn followed her aunt into the kitchen. She banged the door violently behind her her and without bothering to lower her voice said, 'Aunt Margaret, you haven't asked him to stay here?'

'It's only for one night, love.' Gammy's voice was at its most persuasive. 'He was staying at old Mogey's farm, and you know what that's like. I wouldn't wish it on my worst enemy.'

'Where's he sleeping?' demanded Taryn. 'On the settee? He won't find it very comfortable.' The idea of Luke's six foot curled on the two-seater caused her to smile drily.

Gammy concentrated on setting out cups and saucers with minute precision. 'I thought that perhaps he could have your room—you can sleep with me.'

'Over my dead body!' Taryn's voice rose even higher. 'Why should I give up my bed for a man I don't even like? I think you might have consulted me before asking him.'

'Well, it's too late now,' retaliated her aunt. 'I can't go back on my word.'

'Then I'm going to Janice's. I won't stay here—with him.'

'Taryn——' began Gammy, when the door opened.

Luke looked worried. 'I couldn't help overhearing. If it's inconvenient I'll go. It's not too——'

'Oh, no,' insisted Gammy. 'Taryn's just being awkward. You're *my* guest. You must stay.'

'We—ll—' He hesitated and waited for Taryn's reaction.

She glared at him. 'I'm surprised you accepted, knowing how I feel. But I won't be so unkind as to say you can't stay.'

'I thought that perhaps you'd got over your little outburst by now,' he said, 'but if it will make you feel any easier I'll willingly sleep down here.'

Gammy spoke at once. 'I won't hear of it.'

Taryn said, 'On the settee?'

Luke's eyebrows lifted slightly and a gleam of amusement came into his eye. 'I've slept in worse places. I can manage. I wouldn't dream of turning a lady out of her bed.'

Taryn coloured, but before she could speak her aunt said, 'We'll borrow Robert's camp bed. Run along and ask him, Taryn.'

'I'll come with you,' volunteered Luke. 'Who's Robert? A friend of yours?'

'My brother,' said Taryn sharply. 'Rory's father.'

'Then I'm sure he won't mind.' Luke had the door open and they stepped out together. It was dark now, the only light the shimmering half moon and a multitude of stars. As Taryn stumbled over a loose stone Luke's arm caught her waist, steadied her, and stopped there. Taryn stiffened, while at the same time the sudden racing of her heartbeats confirmed an idea that had been forming in her mind ever since Luke kissed her. She couldn't fool herself any longer that her feelings for Mark Vandyke were dead. If she hated him as much as she told herself was it likely that a man who looked so very much like him would stir her senses like this? If she hated Mark she would hate Luke too. It was logical. So—her love for Mark was still there, and this man—whether he really was her fiancé or whether he was his double—was capable of arousing this emotion.

He felt the tensing of her young body. 'You need have no fear,' he murmured gruffly, 'I have no ulterior motives.'

'I never thought you had,' defended Taryn.

'Then why resist me?'

'Am I?' Taryn injected surprise into her voice.

'You know damn well you are,' came the terse reply. 'You've resisted me right from the beginning, and I'm getting a teeny bit tired of the situation. You can't guess what it's like to be condemned for something you haven't done.'

'I'm sorry.' Taryn's response surprised herself. 'I

74

do mean to try—it's just that—that when I'm with you it's like being with Mark, and then I remember what he did to me and I can't help myself.'

'You'll have to get over him some time. You can't go on like this for ever.'

'I know, but it's easier said than done. I keep telling myself I'm being stupid, but——' she faltered, not knowing how to go on.

'You see me and forget your good intentions?' His voice told her he was smiling.

'You're very patient. I don't know why you don't find someone else to do your work. I seem to make a habit of being rude to you.'

He turned his head towards her. She could see the faint gleam of his teeth. 'You interest me,' he said. 'You make a refreshing change from most of the young women I employ.'

'Meaning that you receive deferential treatment from them? Yes, sir; no, sir; three bags full, sir.' She could imagine them—the clerks and receptionists, the waitresses and room maids, all a little in awe of the head of the Major chain of hotels and all a little in love with him.

He chuckled now. 'Something like that. It's very flattering but can become a little monotonous.'

'And I relieve your monotony. Is that a compliment?'

'Most certainly it is. I find you fascinating.'

'Despite my bad temper?'

'Because of it. It's not every day I'm taken for someone else's fiancé. It's very intriguing.'

'Ex-fiancé, if you don't mind.'

75

'As you wish, though I've a feeling you're not as much against him as you say.'

Taryn pulled away from the arm that still encircled her waist and stopped dead in her tracks. 'How do you make that out?' It was one thing to think along these lines herself, but another to have it thrust upon her by a complete stranger.

'Your reactions, my dear girl. Don't deny that your pulses race every time I touch you, that your breath tightens in your throat and you begin to wonder what's the matter.'

Grateful for the darkness that hid her flaming cheeks, Taryn was about to deny his statement when she realised how futile it would be. If he knew so much about her he would also know that she was lying. 'Your perception amazes me,' she said drily. 'How do you know it's not fear that quickens my heartbeats?'

'I think not,' equally drily, 'and I don't flatter myself that your reaction is for me alone—so what else can I think? You still love Mark, whether you realise it or not.'

'Like hell I do,' retorted Taryn, but her voice lacked conviction. 'Would you still love someone who'd made a fool of you?'

'Love doesn't fade easily. It's not like a tap that can be turned on and off at will. We are the prisoners of our emotions and it takes a strong character to banish from our heart a person once loved dearly. Have you that strength, Taryn?'

He was very close to her now. The moon's brilliance cast strong shadows across his face. The expression in his eyes was lost to her, but she could sense that he regarded this subject seriously.

'I thought I had,' she whispered. 'I thought I had forgotten him—until I met you.'

'So you'd welcome him back?'

Taryn shook her head emphatically. 'I might still —love him, but I shall never forgive him—never.'

Luke smiled and gently ran the back of his hand down her cheek. 'I can almost see the sparks flying. I wonder if you really would be so hard.' His hand slid round the back of her neck. 'I don't think so. In fact'—drawing her closer—'I think you might'— his lips brushed her cheek—'have no resistance at all.'

Beneath his touch Taryn felt herself go limp, felt a sudden flaring response. Unable to help herself, she returned his kisses. For a blissful moment all else was forgotten; then in an instant of blinding truth she asked herself what she was doing. Luke was a married man. How could she behave like this? He too, un-less—a horrifying thought—he was experimenting again? She forced her hands up between them and pushed him away. 'And what was that supposed to mean?' Her breathing was uneven and her eyes wide and luminous.

'Merely trying to prove something,' he said lightly, and then on a note of concern, 'You're not offended?'

Taryn's eyes narrowed. 'Would it matter if I was? It doesn't seem to make much difference what I say—you still go your own way.'

'Like staying at the cottage tonight? That wasn't my idea. I fully intended leaving before you got back.'

77

'I'm not sure that I believe you.'

'I'd like you to—it hurts to think that you mistrust me.'

'Very well.' The words were drawn begrudgingly from her. 'I know Gammy can be very insistent.' She began walking towards her brother's house. Her aunt would soon be wondering what was keeping them.

Luke caught her up and held out his hand, 'Friends?'

She couldn't help laughing at his woebegone expression and slid her hand into his, 'Okay, friends.'

Robert's wife, Marjorie, came to the door; she smiled when she saw Taryn. 'Hello, Rory's been telling us what a wonderful day he's had. Oh—you're not alone?' suddenly observing Luke standing behind her. 'Mr Major! How nice to meet you again. Do come in.'

Robert held a pyjama-clad Rory on his lap, but at the sight of their visitors the small boy jumped down, a wide grin on his face. 'Hello, Mr Helicopter man. Aunt Taryn didn't tell me you were here.'

'She didn't know,' responded Luke in a stage whisper. 'It was a surprise visit.'

'So you're Mr Major.' Robert stood up and held out his hand. 'I'm glad to meet you at last. What with young Rory and Taryn I feel I know you already.'

'Luke, please, and I trust you've heard only good about me?'

'From Rory, yes, he talks of nothing else but his ride in your chopper. He's the envy of all the kids at school.'

'But Taryn's story was different, eh?' Luke raised

his brows comically. 'Don't worry, I know all about my resemblance to Mark. What do you think about it. Am I like him?'

Robert shook his head. 'Never met him. It was a whirlwind romance in Italy and the first we knew of it was when Taryn wrote to say she was engaged.'

Rory, who had been listening to this conversation with interest, darted to the sideboard and pulled open a drawer. After searching for a few seconds he found what he wanted. 'Here's a photograph of Uncle Mark,' he announced triumphantly, pushing the thin card into Luke's hand. 'He does look like you, doesn't he?'

Marjorie pounced on the child. 'Rory, I think it's time you were in bed. That was very naughty of you. Aunty Taryn might not want Mr Major to see that picture.'

'It's all right,' smiled Taryn. 'By the way, before you settle Rory down, can we borrow your camp bed? Gammy's invited Luke to stay for the night.'

'Gee, does that mean you'll be here tomorrow?' cut in Rory. 'Can I have another ride?'

'Well now, young man,' said Luke, dropping to one knee beside the boy, 'I reckon we'll have to see about that. I can't possibly take any passengers who are too tired to concentrate. Flying's a serious business. You need your full quota of sleep.'

'I'm going right now,' Rory enthused, darting for the door.

'Then I guess we might manage another short trip tomorrow,' laughed Luke. 'Goodnight.'

Robert followed his son. 'I'll get that bed while I'm up.'

Luke still held the photograph. He glanced at it again now and across to Taryn. 'It's like looking in a mirror. You certainly weren't kidding when you said we were alike.'

'Perhaps now you'll appreciate how I feel,' said Taryn drily.

'I already do, surprising as it may seem.'

Marjorie, sensing the friction between them, suggested they might like a cup of tea.

'Thanks, but no,' smiled Luke. 'We mustn't stay long. Gammy's waiting for us,' and as Robert came down with the bed they said goodbye and returned to Honeysuckle Cottage.

Taryn sat up, startled into sudden wakefulness by a sound that had filled the cottage. She listened again, but all was silent, then a healthy curse in a man's deep voice reached her ears. Luke! What was he doing? Reaching for her dressing gown, she tiptoed down the stairs. The room was in darkness, but a telltale glimmer from beneath the kitchen door gave just enough light for her to see that the camp bed was empty, the blankets tossed into an untidy heap on the floor.

The sound of broken glass being swept up caused her to investigate further. She pushed open the door. Luke was on his hands and knees trying ineffectively to sweep milk and the shattered fragments of a bottle into the dustpan, one hand covered in a handkerchief through which blood was already oozing. He stood up when he saw Taryn. 'Sorry, did I wake you? I couldn't sleep and thought I'd make myself a drink.'

He frowned as she began to giggle.

'So I see,' and she burst into peals of laughter.

Luke looked surprised and then, suddenly realising what was the cause of her amusement, embarrassed. 'Oh, damn,' he said, 'I'd forgotten I was wearing this.' He looked down at the bright pink candlewick dressing gown lent to him by an insistent Gammy. 'It was quicker than dressing, though I wish I had, then I wouldn't have dropped the milk. How can you stand these things flapping round your ankles?'

'I share your abhorrence,' smiled Taryn, indicating her own very short nylon coat.

He followed her gaze and seemed to forget his self-consciousness, for his eyes twinkled. 'I see I was right.'

'About what?'

'Your legs,' he nodded appreciatively.

It was Taryn's turn now to feel uncomfortable, but she hid her confusion by grabbing the brush and proceeding to dispose efficiently of the pieces of glass. A mop next soon cleaned up the milk.

'Don't you think you'd better do something about your hand?' She looking at the spreading stain on his handkerchief.

'Lord, I'd forgotten all about it.' He pulled the linen away and held the offending finger under the tap. Blood still flowed freely.

'I'll get the first aid box.' Taryn filled a basin with water into which she tipped antiseptic and stood it on the table beside him.

'Would you mind?' Luke held out his hand. 'I'm no good with my left.'

Hesitantly Taryn dabbed at the wounded finger,

stopping when he winced. 'Glass!' she said after inspecting the cut more closely. 'It should come out with plenty of water. I'll try not to hurt.' She hoped he would not notice her hands trembling or the fact that her colour had risen. It was difficult to understand why he had this effect on her, but he did, and there was little she could do about it, except try to ignore her emotions and act as though nothing was wrong.

At last, satisfied that the wound was clean, Taryn dried and taped the finger, moving away from his disturbing influence as soon as she could. 'I'll make the drink this time,' she said primly. 'What would you like—tea, coffee, chocolate?'

'Chocolate, please.' He perched himself on the edge of the table and watched as she deftly arranged cups on a tray and filled a saucepan with milk.

Aware of his interest, Taryn grew hotter and hotter and wished she had stopped to pull on trousers and sweater. Luke himself now seemed unconcerned by his own incongruous appearance. His arms were folded against his chest, one bare leg swung to and fro through the opening of the gown. He looks like a proud chieftain, she thought.

'Mark's a very lucky man,' he remarked suddenly.

Taryn eyed him warily. 'Because he found out in time I wouldn't make a suitable wife?'

'Hardly,' laughed Luke. 'Trust you to get hold of the wrong end of the stick! I mean the fact that you still love him after all he's done. It's a special kind of woman who will love her man through thick and thin.'

'I wish you wouldn't insist that I love him. I—I'm not certain how I feel, but I'm darn sure that if he walked into the room right now I wouldn't exactly greet him with open arms.'

'Yet you kissed me, imagining I was Mark—how do you make that out?'

'I didn't,' she retorted hotly. 'I mean—I don't know what came over me, but I can assure you it won't happen again.' Then she saw the twinkle in his eye. 'Oh, stop it, you're insufferable!' and she poured the milk unsteadily into the cups.

'But you do like me?'

She nodded reluctantly.

'Enough to let me take you out tomorrow, or should I say today?' looking at the wall clock which showed half past two.

'Oh, I couldn't—I mean, I'd like to,' she did not want to sound rude, 'but under the circumstances it would hardly seem right.' In point of fact the idea of spending a day with Luke was far more tempting than she cared to admit—but he was married! This made all the difference in the world so far as Taryn was concerned.

'Are you worried about convention?' she scoffed. 'Enjoy yourself, Taryn. Forget other people. You've worked hard this week, you deserve a break—and I must admit I could do with one myself.'

'We—ll, I suppose it will be all right.'

'You don't sound very enthusiastic.'

'It's not because of you, don't get me wrong. I know you'll make sure I enjoy myself.'

'Then you have no excuse. I won't take no for an

answer. Where shall we go?'

Realising she had lost her battle, Taryn smiled and said, 'Seacombe. It's our nearest seaside—very small and very quiet—unless you'd prefer somewhere with more life?'

'No, no. It will suit me fine. I see enough fast living. Do you think Gammy will pack us a lunch?'

'I'll do it myself, though if we don't go back to bed soon I'll never be up to go anywhere.'

They finished their drink in silence. Luke rinsed the cups and left them on the draining board. 'Goodnight, Taryn. I won't disturb you again.'

But it was a long time before she slept. Her vision was disturbed by the man lying downstairs. Of the face she had once tried to forget and which had now come back into her life. In some strange terrifying way it was as though fate was trying to get its revenge. Destiny wanted her to fall in love with this man, regardless of who he was or where he came from.

She was beginning to accept the fact that he was not Mark. Little things—too tiny to be of any significance in themselves—told her he was not the same person. Mark, for instance, would never have slept on a camp bed. He liked his comfort too much. And a quiet day by the sea? Not at all in his line.

Another thing that she was afraid to acknowledge —refused to acknowledge—yet couldn't ignore. Her response to Luke's overtures. It wasn't simply because he looked like Mark, no matter how many times she told herself it was. She definitely felt drawn towards him, whether it was just a physical attraction she was not sure at this stage—but she couldn't easily push to one side the effect he had on her. Whether he was married or not the magnetism was there. She despised herself for falling prey to another man who did not want her—for of course he didn't. He had a wife—who he presumably loved and who he was bringing here to this village—a thought that had not bothered her until now. Any overtures on his part were merely a form of therapy to try and convince her that she still loved Mark. It seemed that no sooner had she got over one man she was thrown right back in and had to start sorting out her life all over again. Yet in spite of these thoughts she looked forward to spending a whole day in his company.

When Taryn awoke the sun was already high in the sky. Jumping out of bed, she looked through the window—just in time to see Luke's helicopter passing overhead. Her first thought was that he had changed his mind and was leaving after all. A tremor of disappointment ran through her—then she remembered his offer to Rory and smiled. He was a kind man. No wonder her nephew had taken to him.

Downstairs Gammy put her breakfast on the table. 'You're late, child,' she said. 'Luke's been up hours. Says you're going to Seacombe today. When did you decide?'

'About two this morning,' smiled Taryn, and in reply to her aunt's raised eyebrows she explained Luke's mishap with the milk.

Gammy laughed. 'Never heard a thing myself.

Eat up now and I'll see what I can find for your lunch.'

An hour later they were on their way. It was a glorious summer day and Taryn felt almost light-hearted. Almost—the only cloud on her horizon being Luke's married status. Determinedly, though, she pushed this thought to the back of her mind—this would be a day to remember.

Luke drove. He looked cramped in the Mini, even with the seat pushed back as far as it would go, but he assured her he was all right. 'You can take a turn later,' he said, 'if I feel too uncomfortable.'

She looked at him now, his crisp white shirt open to the waist, tailored linen slacks, suede shoes. The silver medallion he wore round his neck glinted in the rays of the sun. He turned, aware of Taryn's interest, and smiled. 'Happy?'

'Mmm,' she nodded blissfully, recalling that this time yesterday she had been on her way to Seacombe to escape Luke Major and now here she was going along with him—and enjoying every minute. It was strange how her feelings had changed in a few short hours. 'Who wouldn't be—on such a marvellous day?'

'And with such marvellous company?' his dimple giving away to the humour which accompanied his statement.

'But of course—I like modest men.'

He laughed. 'And I like you. It must be years since I gave myself a day off like this. I'm determined to make the most of it.'

'Surely you have holidays?'

'Of a kind—usually busman's holidays. No, I feel free today. I'm going to forget about work.'

Taryn pulled a face. 'I was going to ask what you thought of the progress at Dale End, but I suppose I'd better keep quiet.'

'That's different—I don't mind talking about the house. It's going to be my retreat—my little hideaway.' He braked quickly to avoid a stray lamb that had wandered across the road. 'I must say I was pleasantly surprised. Andy's raked together some good men, and between them they're working wonders.'

'Do you approve of the decor?'

His mouth twitched. 'Naturally. I knew I would. I told you I trusted your taste.'

'Thank you, kind sir,' said Taryn demurely. 'I can't wait to see the finished result. I've had a whale of a time choosing the furniture and the carpets and the curtains.' She put her head to one side contemplatively. 'You know, I might take up interior designing if this turns out successfully. I rather fancy myself in that role.'

He shot her a sidelong glance. 'In preference to your old job?'

'Definitely. I've come to the conclusion that high fashion is not for me. I don't regret it. My training will still help. It's given me an eye for colour and the blending of colours and textures. It can be applied equally to fabrics or houses.'

'Well said,' applauded Luke. 'If you do decide to change over to interior designing let me know. I might be able to give you a few leads.'

87

An hour later the road led them alongside a river. 'Let's rest a while,' said Luke, stopping the car and stretching his arms lazily above his head. 'They certainly didn't make these cars with tall men in mind.'

'You insisted,' laughed Taryn. 'Come on, let's cross to the other side.'

A series of rocks led to the opposite bank, looking as though they had been put there for that purpose. Taryn took off her sandals and rolled up her jeans. 'In case I slip,' she explained, but Luke, it seemed, had no such qualms. He strode easily from boulder to boulder, pausing occasionally to ensure that Taryn was following safely.

He had almost reached the other side when his foot slipped on a stone that, because it was lower in the water, was covered by a layer of slime. His arms flailed the air in a futile attempt to regain his balance. Taryn started to laugh at the comical picture he presented, but her mirth changed to concern when his hand caught her arm and she went down in the water with him. For a moment they looked at each other in silence. Then Luke's dimples appeared. Suddenly they were both helpless with laughter.

'I'm sorry,' he said, once he had regained his composure. 'You're not hurt?'

'I'm not sure.' Taryn flexed her limbs experimentally. She rubbed her hip. 'A bit sore where I fell, but otherwise fine.'

'Good—but what a sight we look! Shall we go back to the car or lie down in the sun until we dry out?'

'We'll go back. I've brought my swimming gear with me—and a pair of Robert's trunks for you. If we change into those it will save wetting the car. Once we get to Seacombe we can dry our clothes there.'

'Efficient as well as pretty.' His voice held admiration and Taryn felt a warm glow spread through her body. Determinedly she moved away. Nothing must spoil this day—least of all her emotions.

'Do you know,' she called over her shoulder, gingerly retracing her steps, 'this is the same river that runs through our valley?'

Luke stopped and looked upstream with renewed interest. 'In that case we should have come by boat.'

Taryn's laughter mingled with the running waters as they gurgled and bubbled between the boulders. 'I'd like to see you! It runs underground for several miles.'

'Oh, well,' he shrugged, 'it was just a thought. I've never done any boating. It's something I've always promised myself but never found the time to do.'

'We can soon remedy that,' called Taryn. 'I know an old fisherman in Seacombe who might lend us his boat. It's not the height of luxury, but at least it's seaworthy.'

They changed behind the shrubs near the bank of the river. Robert's trunks fitted Luke perfectly and as he turned his back to put his clothes into the car Taryn suddenly realised that here was indisputable proof that he was not Mark. Running diagonally across Mark's back had been a long jagged scar, faded by the years yet still clearly visible. An accident when he was a boy, he had told her, and she had not liked to question him further.

'What's the matter?'

Taryn was unaware that she stood perfectly still staring at Luke's smooth, brown back. 'I've just found out you're not Mark,' she said faintly.

His eyebrows rose until they almost disappeared beneath the brown hair that fell forward over his forehead. 'The times I've denied it! What have I done now to convince you?'

'Mark had a scar—across his back.'

His eyes softened and a wide smile appeared. 'Hallelujah!' Quicker than lightning his arms were about her waist and he twirled her round, laughing delightedly. 'Perhaps now we can get down to the serious business of becoming friends.'

CHAPTER FIVE

TARYN recalled Luke's words as she climbed up to Dale End the next morning. It had been an enjoyable day—one of the best she could recall—but now that he had gone she began to wonder whether it had been a wise thing to encourage him.

She had deliberately pushed all thoughts of his wife to the back of her mind, not a difficult task as Luke never mentioned her. She sometimes wondered why, but did not dwell on it, thankful in a way not to be reminded of what was the only flaw in their relationship.

In every other respect he had proved a delightful companion, teasing, flirting, attentive to her every whim. On the boat he had been like a small boy and had gone so far out that the mainland was a mere speck, returning only when Taryn had implored him not to go any further.

It had been dark when they returned home, and Gammy had already gone to bed. They had crept round the cottage like two burglars not wishing to be caught. For the second night running Luke had slept on the camp bed, but when Taryn woke he had gone.

Gammy asked no questions about their day out, so Taryn presumed Luke must have told her all. She was glad, for she did not feel like discussing Luke with anyone. This new-found friendship was as yet too fragile to be shared, too delicate to even think about—for it had no future. Yet it was impossible not to recall the pleasure this man had given her. In one respect it was like her courtship with Mark all over again and she supposed it was natural to be attracted to someone so like her first love.

At times she found herself thinking it *was* Mark who caught her hand, Mark who playfully kissed the nape of her neck as they threw themselves down on the sands exhausted after a race along the shore. Then on other occasions it could be no one else but Luke. The gift of wild flowers, the exquisitely shaped piece of green glass, worn smooth by years of tidal disturbances, a tiny pink shell which he had said was as delicate as the tips of her ears. This was Luke, a romantic Luke hidden for the biggest part of the time by his professional veneer.

Her affair in Naples had taught her that love comes easily to some people. Mark had said she was the only girl in the world for him, yet within a few short months he had turned to someone else. Now Luke—married, yet carrying on a mild flirtation. As Taryn was fully aware of the situation no harm would be done, so long as she handled it correctly, either to Luke's wife or to her own peace of mind.

It was easier to put her thoughts into order than to carry them out. Even as she neared the house and heard the sound of workmen whistling her mind was for once not on the job in hand, but on the man whose home this would ultimately become. The week stretched emptily ahead. In fact—a startling thought —Luke had not said whether he would be coming down next weekend or not. It could be that he regarded their excursion as a pleasant interlude—indeed he must, for there was no future in their relationship.

Taryn called out a greeting to Andy before mounting the stairs, glancing approvingly at the freshly painted walls. The whole of the upper floor had been redecorated—apart from the two bedrooms which were being converted into bathrooms. The plumbers were due to arrive today to carry out the necessary work.

Taryn had chosen a soft dusky pink bathroom suite for Luke's wife and a deep-piled dove grey carpet. She stood in the doorway of the empty room imagining the finished results. The overall effect should be prettily feminine. For some reason she had gained the impression that the other woman was accustomed to being surrounded by expensive, elegant objects, and was doing her best to create an atmosphere that would prove to be all of these things.

She wandered now into the tower room. The four-poster bed had arrived. In fact all was ready for its new occupant. Taryn herself had polished the windows last week and hung the lacy curtains which matched the drapes on the bed. Here again pink was the predominant colour, ranging in shades from palest rosebud to deep cyclamen, relieved only by the luxurious lilac carpet.

It was a room any woman would be proud to possess, and Taryn lingered a while before passing next door into Luke's quarters. She had encountered difficulty here, not really knowing what he would like. Eventually she had chosen a tobacco brown carpet, cream walls and a deeper cream bed-cover. Heavy curtains in moss green added a touch of colour and the whole was a pleasing woodland effect.

Sighing deeply, Taryn went downstairs and sought out Andy. 'I think I'll go into Exeter,' she said. 'They still haven't delivered those red curtains I ordered for Luke's study.'

Andy's shaggy brows rose in surprise. 'There's plenty of time, lass. We haven't started in there yet.'

But Taryn felt she must get out of the house. It had suddenly assumed claustrophobic tendencies which threatened to stifle her if she did not escape. The thought of Luke sharing this house with a woman who was as yet an unknown quantity filled her with distaste. 'I know,' she said, 'but there are other things I need, unless you want me here?'

Andy shook his head. 'Not at all. Everything's going perfectly. I must say they're a willing lot of workers —I've never known a job done so quickly. Mind you, with the wages the gaffer's paying them they should work hard. He's even added a bonus if the house is ready within three weeks.'

'Three weeks?' Taryn looked at Andy incredulously. Luke had said nothing to her about being in a hurry to move in.

'That's right. The gaffer doesn't believe in hanging about.'

Taryn's face was thoughtful as she made her way back down the hill. Andy's news had been a shock to her. This meant that in a little over a week's time her work would be finished. Her association with Luke

Major would come to an end, for it was unthinkable that she would see him once his wife lived here.

At the bridge she paused, leaning her elbows on the crumbling stone wall and staring sadly into the slow-moving waters. Why did life always treat her so unfairly?

Suddenly she heard her aunt calling urgently. Racing towards the cottage, she saw Gammy's white face. 'It's Janice,' she called almost before Taryn was within hearing distance. 'She's had a fall. We must get her to hospital.'

'Where's Trevor?'

'Plymouth. There's no way of getting hold of him. If we send for an ambulance it might be too late. I'm afraid she's going to lose the baby. Will you take her, Taryn?'

'Of course.' Taryn was already pulling the key from her bag. Within seconds the car was moving towards her cousin's cottage. Inside she found Janice sitting in an armchair, her face devoid of colour and drawn with pain.

'Please tell me the baby's going to be all right,' Janice implored. 'I think I'll die if I lose him now.'

Taryn murmured a few sympathetic words as between them she and Gammy helped her out to the car. The roads were fairly quiet on this Monday morning and Taryn was able to make good time. Gammy held her granddaughter's hand and spoke encouragingly, but Taryn knew she was desperately worried, both for the sake of Janice and the unborn child.

At the hospital Janice was immediately admitted.

There was nothing Taryn or her aunt could do now except wait. One hour passed and then two. They were informed that an operation was necessary if the baby's life was to be saved—and then, joy of joys, a smiling nurse told them that Janice had a son. Gammy was unashamedly crying and Taryn felt the prick of tears at the back of her eyes.

'And Janice?' whispered Gammy.

'Fine,' nodded the nurse. 'You have no need to worry.'

'Can we see her?' asked Gammy next.

'For a few minutes. She's only just come round from the anaesthetic. She's still dazed, you understand?'

Dazed or not Janice, smiled at them as they approached her bed. 'I've done it,' she said, 'I've given Trevor his son. Poor little mite, he's so tiny. They've put him in an incubator. Oh, Gammy, you will tell Trevor the minute he gets home?'

'Taryn will,' nodded her grandmother. 'I'm staying here.'

It was mid-afternoon before Taryn eventually left the hospital, and as she had had nothing to eat since breakfast she decided to have a coffee and a sandwich before starting the journey back.

For the last few hours Taryn had forgotten all about her own troubles, but now, as she sipped the hot coffee and gazed morosely into the creamy liquid, memory returned. Why does it always happen to me? she pondered. Why can't I——? She never finished her sentence. A gentle hand touched her shoulder. Startled, she swung round. 'Luke! What are you doing here?' She took no trouble to hide her delight.

'Hoping to find you,' he smiled. 'You didn't really think I'd go without saying goodbye? I had to make a short trip, but by the time I got back Andy told me you'd left for Exeter.'

'I thought it strange,' admitted Taryn, 'but how did you know I was in here?'

'I didn't. I'd admitted defeat and was going to have one last coffee before returning to London. Did you get your curtain material?'

'What?' She looked at him blankly. 'Oh, that. No, I've been at the hospital.' And she proceeded to relate the events of the day.

'So now you have to dash back to Ferndale to tell her husband?'

'That's right.'

'Then why are we waiting? Let's go!'

'But I thought you were going back to London?'

'Let's say something more urgent has cropped up.' The meaning behind his words was clear as he smiled down into her eyes, and his hand beneath her arm as they left the restaurant seemed to burn into her flesh.

'I'll drive,' he said as they approached the car. Wordlessly Taryn passed him the key. How difficult it would be to get this man out of her mind, and why was he treating her so—intimately?

Suddenly she noticed they were travelling in the wrong direction. 'Hey,' she said, 'where are we going?'

'My 'copter's not far away. It will be quicker. I'll

get someone to fetch your car later.'

Taryn sat upright in her seat. 'But I couldn't! I mean, is it safe?'

He laughed. 'Of course it's safe. You've flown before. What are you worried about?'

She swallowed. 'There's a lot of difference between a Boeing and your helicopter. It looks so fragile.'

He slanted her a reassuring smile. 'I've travelled hundreds—no, it must be thousands of miles in her. She's never failed me yet.'

'There's always a first time,' replied Taryn faintly.

'You surprise me. Have you no faith?'

'Yes—but——'

He caught her hand, squeezing her fingers gently. 'Dearest Taryn. I'll see no harm comes to you.'

Taryn's heart beat uncomfortably fast. She wanted to withdraw her hand, but she was afraid of hurting his feelings. He spoke as though she really meant something to him. Why? What game was he playing?

Intercepting her puzzled look, he remarked, 'Now what's the matter? Don't you believe me?'

'Yes—it's just me. I'm being silly.'

By this time they had reached the field where his craft was waiting. Without giving her further time to argue Luke was out of the car. He held her hand as they walked towards the helicopter.

Taryn looked fearfully at its gleaming bodywork and bit her lip anxiously. Her heart beat so loud she was sure Luke must hear it and once inside she was even more afraid. After he had started the engine and the blades began to whirr overhead it was too noisy even to talk without shouting. He passed her a pair of earphones, turning round to smile reassuringly, and before she knew it the ground was falling away beneath them.

Suddenly she was enjoying herself. The sensation was so different from what she had expected. It was as though they were being gently lifted into the sky, then propelled slowly forward. It was as though they were floating above the earth and as they climbed higher they hardly seemed to be moving at all. Taryn leaned back in her seat and relaxed, watching the patchwork of fields slide away below.

It seemed no time at all before she saw Ferndale rising to meet them. From this angle it looked so different—like a model village, everything in miniature but in perfect scale. As they lost height Dale End grew larger and larger. The row of cottages reassumed their identity.

They landed safely in the top field, but as they climbed out Taryn was surprised to find how wobbly her legs were and was glad of Luke's supporting hand. 'Everyone feels like that on their first flight,' he said kindly. 'You'll be all right in a minute. Hang on to me.'

She was still holding his arm when they reached Janice's cottage. At the same time Trevor pulled up in his car. He cast them a speculative glance, but before he could speak Taryn said, 'Congratulations, Trevor. You're a father at last!'

He frowned and looked towards the house. 'I can't be—Janice was all right when I left. She's another month yet—where is she?' and he began running towards the door.

'She's not there,' Taryn called out. 'She had a fall.' He stopped and looked back in concern. 'Don't worry, she's perfectly okay. Your son's beautiful.'

'My son!' Trevor said the words proudly, experimentally. 'I must go. Where is she—Exeter?'

Taryn nodded. 'At the——'

Trevor was already climbing back into his car.

'Be careful,' she called, 'mind how you go,' but her words were lost as his wheels spun the gravel and he disappeared in a cloud of dust.

'A cup of tea would be very welcome now,' said Luke, heading in the direction of Honeysuckle Cottage.

The idea of being alone in the cottage with Luke was both tantalising and frightening. Taryn wanted desperately to be near him—but was it wise? He gave every indication that he no longer treated her as an employee. In fact, he seemed to find her very desirable. Under these circumstances would it be prudent to take him home? On the other hand, if she refused he would think it childish. After all, he had gone out of his way to bring her back here and Gammy would expect her to reward his kindness. 'Me, too,' she said hesitantly. 'It's been rather an exhausting day.'

Once inside Taryn was even more aware of Luke's presence. His height dwarfed the already small rooms and when he offered to help in the kitchen it was inevitable that their bodies should touch.

'Would you like something to eat?' asked Taryn breathlessly, more for something to say than because she was hungry herself. If things had been different she would have enjoyed Luke's company; as it was, her whole body was on edge, wondering whether he would take advantage of the situation—even wanting him to. She curled her fingers in her palms to try and still their trembling. He must not see the effect his presence had on her.

'I thought you'd never ask,' he mocked, apparently unaware of her tension.

'Sorry,' she grimaced. 'It was thoughtless of me. How about a salad? There's some cold chicken in the fridge, and one of Gammy's apple pies to follow.'

'Sounds great. I'll go and get a lettuce.'

Whistling softly to himself, he disappeared into the garden and Taryn took the opportunity of the few moments she was alone to try and pull herself together. What's the matter? she chided. Luke's given no indication that he has any ulterior motive in inviting himself here. You're behaving like a lovesick schoolgirl instead of a responsible adult. In any case, surely you know how to handle him should he try any funny business? Of course she did. She was worrying for nothing. It wasn't the first time they had been alone, and nothing had happened before—so why was she working herself up into such a state now?

'Here we are.' Luke dropped the lettuce into the sink and turned on the tap. 'Come on, slowcoach,' he called over his shoulder, 'you've done nothing while I was away.'

Taryn smiled. 'I was thinking how strange it was to have you here like this.'

'You don't mind?'

'Of course not,' she lied. 'Gammy would expect it of me.'

'So you're entertaining me purely to please your aunt?'

'Don't be silly,' retorted Taryn before she noticed the dimple in his cheek. 'Oh, stop making fun of me!'

'Would you like me to do something else?' He didn't look round again, but his deepening voice told her what he had in mind.

'I don't know what you mean,' she said primly.

'I think you do.' He looked at her now, but at her startled expression he laughed suddenly and flicked a wet lettuce leaf in her direction. 'Don't worry, I'm too hungry to think of other things. Anyway, what's got into you today? You seem different. I haven't done anything to upset you?'

Taryn shook her head. 'It's probably because of Janice. I don't like hospitals very much.'

He looked relieved. 'I should have known. What shall I do next?' He piled the lettuce into a dish and stood it on the table. 'Slice the tomatoes?'

'There's no need—really, I can manage.'

'I like helping,' he insisted. 'It's sort of cosy doing things together. I never knew domesticity could be such fun.'

She wondered whether he ever helped his wife. Or whether he was away from home so often that the opportunity never arose. It was a peculiar state of affairs.

At last the meal was ready. They carried it into the living room and arranged it on the table near the window. Dale End was in full view from this point and as Taryn poured their tea she noticed the way Luke kept looking up towards the house. 'I wonder if the plumbers came?' she mused.

Luke nodded. 'They were there this morning. I really must congratulate you on the way things are turning out. It's better than I dared hope.'

'I'm pleased myself.' Taryn's face turned pink under his approval. 'And I just love Mrs Major's room,' she continued in a rush. 'Do you think she'll like it?'

'Without a doubt. When we move in you must come up and let her congratulate you herself. I think you'll get on well together.'

Taryn lifted her brows at this profound statement, but declined to comment, concentrating instead on picking her chicken bone.

Luke himself, unaware of her reaction, continued, 'It's strange you should choose pink. It's always been one of her favourite colours. I remember——'

'How about *your* room?' cut in Taryn shortly, unable to stand hearing him talk about his wife.

He waved his fork expressively. 'Delightful—absolutely perfect—I can say no more. Your tastes are exquisite, my dear Taryn.'

'You flatter me.'

'No, I mean it. I can see that by the time you've finished I shall be unable to tear myself away.'

'Then don't,' she said. 'Surely your hotels will run themselves? You have managers?'

'Naturally, but other people are not so conscientious as oneself. I like to keep them on their toes.'

They finished their meal in silence after that, but

103

it was a comfortable quiet and Taryn could not help but think how wonderful it would be to spend the rest of her life with this man. They understood each other so well; there was an affinity between them that needed no words. In fact, if he spoke now, it would ruin everything. This was how love should be —relaxing, undemanding, perfect union.

Not until Luke waved a hand before her face did Taryn realise she had been staring at him.

'Penny for them,' he smiled.

'They're not worth it.'

'Try me.'

'They're too private.' She jumped up and began stacking their empty plates on to a tray.

Immediately he began to help, but when his hand accidentally touched hers and she backed sharply away he said, 'Taryn, something *is* wrong. You must tell me.'

She turned away, but he caught her shoulders and forced her to face him. With one finger he lifted her chin until she looked into his eyes. 'Now,' he said sternly, 'what is this all about?'

But how could she declare her love—tell him that the thought of his wife tormented her? He had given no true indication that he returned her feelings. He found her good company, desirable even—as a woman, but he did not love her. She could not risk making a fool of herself, so instead she stiffened and said in a tight little voice, 'You're making a mistake. Why should there be anything the matter?'

'I'm asking *you* that.'

'Then I can only say you've got the wrong impression.' She wriggled free. 'I'm going to wash up now. Isn't it time you were going?'

'Now I know there's something amiss. What is it? Are you afraid of me? Afraid I might take advantage?' He watched her face closely and saw the involuntary flickering of her eyes. 'Now we're getting somewhere. Have I ever given you reason for such thoughts?' He caught her arms and shook her roughly. 'Have I?'

'You know you haven't,' cried Taryn. 'I can't help how I feel.'

'Or is it that damn Mark fellow?' he grated. 'You're classing me with him. I don't suppose you objected when *he* put his arms round you; when *he* pulled you close and suffocated you with kisses, but you don't want *me* to, is that it? Don't you know I'm human the same as him? That I'm attracted to you the way he was?'

Taryn shook her head dumbly. 'You—you don't understand.'

'I understand only too well,' he rasped. 'Believe me, I'm getting a little sick and fed up of having your past lover rammed down my throat.'

'You brought him up,' retorted Taryn.

'But he was in your thoughts, which is the same thing. I think I will go after all. I suddenly feel the need for some fresh air.'

He had reached the door before Taryn spoke. 'Luke, please—I didn't mean to upset you.' She hadn't meant to say that either—the words had been torn from her.

Luke stopped and slowly turned. He looked defeated and with a little cry Taryn ran towards him.

He held her tightly and she could feel the unsteady beating of his heart and the lean strength of his thighs against hers. She lifted her head and his lips came down on hers, crushing and bruising. But she cared no longer. If his wife didn't want him here was one woman who did. Her hands crept up behind his neck, her fingers tangling in his hair and pulling his head even more tightly towards her. She felt curiously abandoned. Never before had she felt so moved, even with Mark. His kisses had aroused her, oh yes, but never anything like this. She gave a moan of pleasure and at once Luke lifted his head. 'Am I hurting you?'

Taryn shook her head. Almost immediately his lips sought hers again, straining her to him until she felt as though she must suffocate.

At length he stopped, but he did not let her go. Instead he led her to the settee where they sat together, she nestling in the crook of his arm and Luke's head resting on top of hers. 'No regrets?' he asked softly.

'None at all,' whispered Taryn.

'I didn't really mean that to happen, but I won't say I'm sorry.'

She could tell by his voice that he was smiling, could imagine the dimple in his cheek and the softening of his eyes. 'Nor me,' she answered.

There was a long silence during which neither of them stirred. It was Luke himself who made the first move. 'I suppose I must go,' he said, gently lifting her away.

'Stay the night,' she ventured. 'I'm sure Gammy

won't mind.'

'I know, but I must leave. I have an appointment in London first thing in the morning.'

'When will you come again?' asked Taryn anxiously, suddenly realising that she was going to miss him.

'I have to go up north at the end of the week,' he said sadly, 'so it will be the weekend after before I get down.'

'Oh.' The house would be finished by then, thought Taryn, her brief affair would be over.

'Why do you say "Oh," like that?' he asked, smiling.

Taryn shrugged. 'It seems such a long time.'

'I'm sure you'll find plenty to do—and it's not so long really. I'll be thinking of you, Taryn.'

Her voice was wistful. 'Will you?'

'But of course. Now I really must go.'

She accompanied him to the door. He kissed her tenderly, then walked away down the valley. Taryn watched him go. She might never see him alone again. Next time—if the house was ready—he could bring his wife with him. Abruptly she decided to make sure that the house was not finished in the three weeks he had stipulated. She wasn't sure what she was going to do at this stage, but she would think of something—anything to delay the time when Mr and Mrs Major moved into Dale End.

CHAPTER SIX

GAMMY observed Taryn shrewdly when she came down to breakfast the next morning. 'You look as though you've had a bad night. What's the matter?'

'It's Luke,' she said reluctantly while realising that her aunt would find out sooner or later. 'We met in Exeter and he came back here last night.'

'So?' prompted Gammy. 'Why should that cause any problems?'

'I think I'm in love with him,' replied Taryn candidly. 'I tried not to—but I couldn't help myself.'

'It's the rainbow,' decisively. 'What did I tell you?'

'But have you forgotten he's married?'

Gammy pulled a face. 'Has he actually told you so?'

'We—ll, no, but according to Andy——'

'Wait until he tells you himself before you condemn the man,' interrupted her aunt firmly. 'He doesn't strike me as the sort to deceive anyone—least of all you.'

'And what is that supposed to mean?'

'It's quite obvious he's attracted by you. Why don't you ask whether he's married? He probably has no idea what's on your mind.'

'I'll see,' murmured Taryn, but she had no intention of so doing. It was not the sort of question she could ask Luke. If he did not volunteer any information about his personal life who was she to pry? If only she hadn't fallen in love. She had managed to survive one heartbreak—but two? It didn't bear thinking about.

Immediately after breakfast Taryn made her way up to Dale End. Work was still in full swing and she threw herself wholeheartedly into polishing windows and hanging curtains—a job that she was not obliged to do but one which successfully took her mind off the man who had disrupted her life.

Time dragged interminably during the following days, Taryn's only consolation the transformation of the house. By the end of the second week the redecorating was complete. All that remained was for the carpets and the rest of the furniture to arrive. As if in answer to her prayers there had been some trouble with the suppliers and it was to be a further seven days before the final touches could be put to Dale End. By Friday evening Taryn had worked herself into a state of nervous exhaustion until even Gammy lost patience and rated her soundly.

And as the weekend passed with no sign of Luke, not even a message to say that he had been delayed, Taryn knew that she was making herself ill for nothing. If he returned her feelings surely he would have found some way of contacting her?

On Monday morning there was no work to do in the house. The men had left, including Andy. Taryn wandered listlessly from room to room, for once experiencing no joy in its newly acquired charm. Eventually she went out into the garden and finding tools in one of the outhouses began to weed the borders from which the roses grew so rampantly along the portico.

So engrossed did Taryn become in her work that she did not hear the sound of a car or soft footsteps approaching. When a hand touched her shoulder she jumped so violently that her hand fell against one of the stems, causing a thorn to drag across the back of her hand and leaving a thin red line in its wake.

Involuntarily she cried out, but the pain was forgotten when she looked up into the tawny eyes regarding her with concern.

'I'm sorry,' said Luke. 'I shouldn't have surprised you like that. Are you hurt badly?'

'It's nothing.' Taryn was more conscious of her dishevelled appearance. She had on a pair of her oldest jeans and a sleeveless sweater that had seen better days. It had risen up as she worked to reveal a bare expanse of flesh, and she now tugged it down self-consciously.

His eyes twinkled. 'I've seen you in less. Why the modesty?'

But Taryn ignored his bantering tones. 'I'm sorry I'm not ready,' she said drily. 'You should have let me know you were coming.'

In reality she wanted to fling herself into his arms and declare her pleasure at seeing him again. But when she recalled that for two whole weeks he had made no attempt to get in touch with her she knew that he did not regard her in exactly the same way. It could be embarrassing, for it became clear to her now that he had only been filling in the time until his wife was installed at Dale End. He was no better than any other man who, given the opportunity, would not hesitate to indulge in a light flirtation. On this account alone she must keep a tight rein on her feelings, and although it hurt to assume an air of indifference it was the only way she could survive their meetings without revealing her true emotions.

'Hey, what is this? What have I done to deserve such treatment?'

Taryn's eyes fell before his questioning gaze and she returned once again to the work in hand, but he hooked a hand beneath her arm and pulled her up.

'If it's because I didn't get here for the weekend,' he said, 'I'm sorry. I got held up.'

'Why should that bother me? It's none of my business what you do.'

'If it upsets you, then it is. If I'd known I'd have found some way of letting you know.'

Taryn struggled from his grasp, still loth to let him believe she was disturbed. 'It doesn't matter.'

'Then what's happened to the happy girl I left behind? Not brooding over Mark again? I thought I'd managed to push him out of your mind for good.'

You have, you have, cried Taryn to herself, but aloud she said, 'I haven't been sleeping too well, that's all.' She couldn't go on denying there was nothing wrong, and at least this was the truth.

Luke frowned. 'Then why aren't you resting? There's no need for you to do this,' indicating the garden with an expressive wave of his hand, 'I'm employing a full-time gardener. Come on, let's go inside.' He led her into the kitchen. 'To quote your aunt, a good strong cup of tea is what you need. Sit down while I do the honours.'

Taryn watched silently as Luke made the tea. She was very aware of the fact that there was only the two of them in the house, and recalled the last occasion they had been in just such a position. Her skin tingled at the thought of his lips against hers and a sudden warmth pervaded her body. Abruptly she crossed to the window and flung it wide open, breathing in deeply the light summer air. She would never rid herself of her fascination for this man—no matter how much she told herself it was wrong.

Luke glanced at her curiously but said nothing. He finished pouring the tea, then came and stood behind her. 'I wish I understood you, Taryn. You act very strangely sometimes.'

Her heart beat wildly at the feel of his body against hers. She tried to move, but his arms imprisoned her tightly.

'You're behaving as though we're strangers again. I really thought that at last I was getting somewhere, that you'd forgotten all this nonsense about Mark.'

Taryn jerked her head round to look at him. 'I scarcely think of him these days.'

'Then you *are* annoyed with me. Oh, Taryn,' he twisted her round to face him, 'if only you knew how many times I've wanted to see you! If you'd been on the phone I'd have called every day, as it was I had to content myself with thinking about you.' His eyes searched her face as if looking for some tiny detail he might have missed. 'Every night you've filled my dreams.'

'Please——' protested Taryn, but he ignored her cry.

'Every morning I've woken and deplored the thought of another day without seeing you. But never mind, I intend delegating some of my work after all and spending as much time here as I can. I'm training a new man now and once the house is finished I hope to be here every weekend, more often if possible.'

Taryn closed her eyes. It was a tantalising thought, but didn't he realise that once the house was finished her job would be over too? And as she couldn't go on living off Aunt Margaret for ever she would have to find another job, which in its turn meant moving out of the valley. This really was the end. Another week at the most was all she could expect, yet Luke was talking as though the whole future stretched before them.

'I can see you don't believe me,' he said softly. 'I'm truly serious, Taryn. I've missed you more than I thought possible.'

'Me, too.' Taryn's voice was scarcely more than a whisper, but Luke heard and crushed her relentlessly to him.

'Taryn,' he breathed hoarsely, 'dearest Taryn.' He wrapped her hair round his fingers and roughly pulled her head back. His eyes were as dark as coals when he kissed her. There was a pain in their depths such as Taryn had never seen before. She knew she ought to resist, but her desire matched his and she returned his kisses with a wanton urgency that surprised even herself. His lips moved to her throat and her ears and her eyes. Her hands crept up round his neck and she pressed herself against him. This was probably the last time they would be together and she felt as though she never wanted to let him go.

At length it was Luke himself who released her and stumbled away to grope for a chair. He ran a hand through his hair and looked at her with glazed eyes. 'What have I done? It's all wrong. I should never——'

'Shh!' she whispered, placing a finger across his lips. 'Don't blame yourself. I wanted you to kiss me.'

Hungrily he caught her hand and pressed kisses into its palm. 'I didn't want this to happen—not yet—but when I'm with you I can't help myself.' He pulled her down on to his lap. 'Forgive me?'

'There's nothing to forgive,' Taryn sighed, curling her arm round his neck. 'We're both human. It was inevitable.'

'All the same, I'm sorry. I had no right.'

Silence settled over them and Taryn guessed that he too was thinking of his wife and the wrong they were doing her. It was no good; she would have to leave the valley. For the second time in her short life running away seemed to be the only solution.

They drank their tea and Taryn washed up. Luke then suggested they go into Exeter to see if they couldn't speed up delivery of the remainder of the furnishings.

'I've promised to take Janice to fetch the baby home,' declared Taryn ruefully.

'That's no problem,' was his cheerful reply. 'We'll all go together. I'm sure my car will be more comfortable than the Mini. What time are you going?'

'About two—but really, Luke, I'd far rather——'

He held up his hand. 'No arguing. I shall be delighted to help, but first of all we must think about lunch. There's no food here, of course?'

Taryn shook her head. 'I didn't realise you expected me to——'

He laughed. 'Of course not. I expect Helen will want to see to all that herself. How about your aunt? Dare I intrude once more?'

'Intrude?' Taryn tried to match his easy tones. 'She'll be offended if she knows you've been here and not called in to see her.' But all the time she spoke her mind was on the word Helen. It was the first time he had called her by name. It conjured up a picture of a gentle, faithful woman who never let her husband down, and it made Taryn all the more determined to put an end to their relationship. After today there must be no more meetings without a third person present. Only in that way could they avoid the inevitable attraction they both felt for each other.

As Taryn had expected Gammy was delighted to see Luke and lunch was a very lighthearted affair. Afterwards they picked up Janice, who had completely recovered from her operation and was anxious to bring her baby home. It was the first time her cousin had met Luke and Taryn was amused by her open curiosity.

The rest of the day passed uneventfully—due no doubt to Janice's restraining presence, but Taryn was grateful they had no opportunity for any more personal conversation between herself and Luke. On the way back he told her he had managed to arrange delivery of the carpets and furniture for the following day. How he had managed to influence them when she herself had argued in vain, Taryn did not know, but the fact remained that by tomorrow evening all would be ready for the Majors to move in. Taryn was saddened by this thought and when he left later in the evening she felt as though her world had come to an end.

True to their word, the carpet fitters arrived mid-morning the next day and later in the afternoon the furniture was delivered. Soon everything was in order. Taryn took one last lingering look round the place, felt an overwhelming satisfaction in a job well done, but a consuming sadness that this would most likely be the last time she set foot inside Dale End.

Wednesday and Thursday went by with no evidence of anyone moving into the big house. Then on Friday Taryn saw Luke's white Volvo parked in the drive. So he had arrived—and presumably Helen Major with him.

Taryn slept little that night.

On Saturday she took Gammy into Plymouth for a shopping expedition. 'While I still have the car,' she joked. 'Luke's sure to want it returning to the hire company now that I've finished.'

It was Sunday morning before she encountered Luke again. On her return from exercising Dainty she saw him striding down the hill. Her heart fluttered painfully and she turned away towards the cottage, anxious to put off this final meeting for as long as possible.

She was washing her hands in the kitchen when Gammy ushered Luke in. 'Hello, Taryn,' he smiled. 'I've been expecting you up at the house.'

'Oh, I couldn't,' she said, trying to ignore the sudden racing of her pulses. 'Not without an invitation. I mean, my job's finished now. It would be intruding.'

'Don't be silly. Helen wants to meet you. In fact that's why I'm here now, to invite you and Gammy to lunch.'

'How very kind of her,' exclaimed Gammy before Taryn could speak. 'We'd be delighted, if you're sure it's no trouble. You've hardly had time to settle in.'

Luke grinned comfortably. 'Helen's made herself at home already. She adores the place—I knew she would—and she insists on congratulating you personally, Taryn.'

The girl could hardly refuse now, yet she wished with all her heart that she did not have to go. It would be extremely difficult to hide her feelings from Luke's wife—one of the most difficult tasks ever imposed upon her. 'I'm glad,' she said politely. 'I look forward to meeting her.'

Luke stayed a few minutes longer before announcing that he must rush back. 'I have to help Helen with the chores,' he laughed. 'She wants everything just right for her first visitors. You know what women are like.'

'She doesn't expect to run the house on her own?' queried Gammy.

'Gosh, no. She's looking round for a housekeeper and probably a daily woman as well. If you know of anyone suitable please let her know, she'll be very grateful.'

After he had gone Taryn said to Gammy, 'I wish you hadn't accepted. I don't want to meet Luke's wife.'

'Rubbish,' snorted her aunt. 'It's got to happen some time, so the sooner the better. At least you'll have me to support you.'

Taryn pulled a face. 'I'll need it. For goodness' sake don't leave us alone together in case she probes my relationship with Luke.'

'Why should she, unless you give her cause for suspicion? It's a pity he's married—and there seems no doubt about it now. I like Luke and I was sure that——'

'We were made for each other,' finished Taryn with a smile. 'It doesn't look as though your rainbow's working this time, Gammy dear.'

Her aunt sighed. 'It's never been wrong yet,' and with a swift change of subject, 'I must say I'm looking forward to seeing Dale End. You've told me so much I feel I know it already.'

'It's beautiful,' sighed Taryn dreamily. 'I wish it was mine.'

As she lay soaking in her bath a little while later Taryn again reflected on the delights of living at Dale End, and more especially so as Luke's wife. Then she scolded herself for entertaining such irrational thoughts. It was a dream that would never come true, so it was madness to even think about it.

She jumped out and vigorously towelled herself dry. She must squash all thoughts of Luke from her

118

mind. It was no use prolonging the agony. Tomorrow she would see about finding herself another job.

She dressed with care in a white crochet trouser suit which she felt was eminently suitable for lunch at Dale End. She was almost ready when Gammy popped her head round the door. 'As I thought,' exclaimed her aunt disgustedly, 'trousers again! Why don't you remember you're a woman and dress in something a little more appropriate?'

'What's wrong with this?' Taryn studied her reflection in the mirror. 'It's very dressy.'

Her aunt stepped into the room. 'For once I'm going to insist. It's not very often I tell you what to do, but this time I mean to have my way.'

'You know I have nothing suitable,' protested Taryn. She felt comfortable in trousers and now she was ready did not want to go to the trouble of changing.

'How about that green silk you brought back from Italy? You haven't worn it since you came home. It will be ideal for today.' Gammy already had Taryn's wardrobe open. 'Here we are. Put that on—and don't be too long. It's almost time to go.'

Taryn hadn't the heart to object again. As her aunt had said, she rarely laid down the law, so it wouldn't hurt to humour her on this occasion.

The dress had been designed by Mark especially for Taryn—one of the reasons why she never wore it now. But once she had slipped into the cool, apple-green material she knew that her aunt was right. It was a beautiful dress and suited her perfectly. The scoop neckline revealed her honey gold tan, the close-fitting bodice emphasised her firm young figure and the full skirt swirled about her legs. She felt like a million dollars, and had it not been for the fact that Mark had always adored her in this dress she would not have minded wearing it now. As it was, painful memories were renewed. Quickly she smoothed down her shoulder-length hair, gave one last critical look at herself in the mirror and left the room.

Gammy was waiting. Her face lit up when she saw her niece. 'Ah,' she exclaimed, 'you look beautiful, my darling. Just one last finishing touch,' and she looped a gold cross and chain round Taryn's neck. 'Your uncle gave me this on the day we were married. I always intended to give it you—when you became a bride—but I'd like you to wear it today.'

Taryn dropped an affectionate kiss on her aunt's cheek and fingered the delicately engraved cross. 'It's beautiful. Thank you.' It moved her almost to tears to think that her aunt had given her one of her most valued possessions.

They went in the car to Dale End, and as Taryn pulled up in front of the house she felt a sudden urge to turn round and go away again. But even as this thought passed through her mind the old oak door opened and Luke came down the steps. He wore a cream linen suit and a tawny brown silk shirt that matched the colour of his eyes. As he came towards them Taryn's heart beat an urgent tattoo in her breast. She licked suddenly dry lips and felt powerless to move. She just sat, watching, as he neared the car. Their eyes met and held and when he opened the door Taryn stepped outside as if in a dream. Luke too appeared stunned. He took a step back and allowed his eyes to cover the whole length of her body, from her neat white sandals to the silky fair hair which, with the sun behind her, framed her face in a shining halo.

'For once I'm at a loss for words,' he said. 'You've always looked good, no matter what you wear, but today——' he shook his head slowly, 'you're like a dream. I'm afraid to touch you in case you disappear.'

Taryn smiled shyly, and put her hand on his arm. 'It really is me,' she said. 'I'm glad you approve.'

Gammy, tired of waiting, suddenly appeared at their side. 'Don't I get a welcome too?'

Instantly Luke swept her into his arms. 'Gammy! I'm sorry, blame your niece. But you look splendid as well.' He held her at arms' length to see more clearly the deep purple dress trimmed with guipure lace at the neck and sleeves. 'Helen and I are honoured to have two such beautiful visitors. Do come in, she'll be wondering where we are.'

Taryn's feet were leaden as she climbed the steps. This was one meeting she dreaded. She glanced at Gammy and received a sympathetic smile in response. Her aunt knew exactly how she felt.

They were now in the tower room, decorated under Taryn's instruction in muted shades of green, verging into blue in the vibrant tones of the deep-piled carpet. The lounge looked cool and inviting, even though flooded with sunshine. A cane screen had been strategically placed to throw shade across one of the easy chairs, though still allowing its occupant a clear view of the valley below. At the sound of

121

their entrance she rose and walked towards them.

Luke stepped forward.

'Taryn, Gammy, I'd like you to meet Helen—my mother.'

There was a long pause during which time Taryn passed from a state of shock to a sense of relief and an overwhelming desire to laugh.

Luke spoke again. 'Helen, this is Taryn.' He said her name with pride.

Helen Major smiled and held out her hand. 'How pleased I am to meet you at last. Luke's told me so much about you, but he certainly didn't do you justice, child. You're far prettier than I expected— and younger too. I can't believe you were responsible for all this.'

Taryn murmured a suitable reply, still dazed by the revelation that Helen was Luke's mother, and while he introduced her to Gammy she studied the other woman with interest. Probably in her late sixties, she had pure white hair, expertly cut to frame her oval face. The lilac dress she wore emphasised the frailness of her body, yet her blue eyes were bright and cheerful and her voice warm and friendly. Taryn liked her instantly and could see the deep affection that existed between mother and son. There was no resemblance between the two of them, so presumably Luke took after his father. She wondered whether he was still alive.

Formalities over, they sat down and Luke poured sherry into sparkling crystal glasses; bringing his own drink over to where Taryn sat and perching on the arm of her chair.

'I trust Luke conveyed my appreciation of all you've done?' Helen smiled. 'Of course I didn't see the place beforehand, but from all I've heard it was in a terrible state.'

'To say the least.' Taryn laughed and looked up at Luke. 'I don't mind admitting it now, but I was pretty scared the first time I came here.'

'Don't I know it,' dimpled Luke, 'but whether it was me or the house I wasn't sure.' His arm rested lightly on her shoulder. 'I'm glad that's all over now.'

Taryn felt swift colour flood her cheeks and looked across to see whether his mother was watching. She need not have worried, for the smile bestowed on her by Helen Major was full of approval. 'What a charming dress,' said the older woman. 'So many young people these days seem to live in jeans that it's a change to find someone proud of her femininity.'

'Thank you, Mrs Major, you're very kind,' acknowledged Taryn, trying to ignore the fact that Luke had choked over his drink and Gammy's lips barely suppressed a smile.

'Helen, please. Luke never calls me anything else and it makes me feel so much younger. Oh, and before I forget, that four-poster bed——'

'You don't like it?' interposed Taryn. 'I was afraid of that, but Luke said——'

'Let me finish,' laughed Helen. 'I've always had a secret longing for one—it's absolutely delightful— and pink—my favourite colour. I had a better night's sleep last night than I've had for years.'

'I'm so pleased.' Taryn felt that the day was going to turn out well after all.

Gammy said, 'Do you think I might have a look over the house? Taryn's told me about it, of course, but I'm longing to see what it's like.'

'I didn't realise you hadn't been here before,' answered Helen immediately. 'I'll take you now, and then I must see how lunch is getting on.'

'Please let me help.' Taryn rose and joined the two women.

'I wouldn't dream of it.' Helen's smile enveloped Luke as well. 'I'm sure you two can find plenty to talk about.'

'Naturally,' rejoined Luke. 'We have unfinished business to discuss.'

As soon as they were alone Taryn said accusingly, 'Why didn't you tell me Helen was your mother?'

Luke's thick brows shot upwards. 'I thought you knew.'

'How could I? You never said.'

'But didn't Andy——?' He shook his head in bewilderment. 'I asked him to tell you which room I wanted for Helen. It was the only one I was really bothered about.'

'He told me all right,' admitted Taryn. 'Mrs Major's room—that's what he said. Now I see why he looked so strange when I asked if you had any children.'

Luke suddenly began to laugh. 'You thought that Helen was——? Oh, Taryn, you silly little goose, why didn't you ask?'

Taryn hung her head. 'How could I? You scarcely mentioned her yourself—and the fact that you had separate rooms. I thought that perhaps everything was not as it should be between you.'

'And that I was playing around with you because I didn't get any love at home?'

'Something like that.'

'If only I'd known! No wonder I didn't seem to be getting anywhere.' He held out his arms and after a moment's hesitation Taryn joined him.

She felt like crying, her relief was so great, She buried her head against his chest and as his arms held her close she suddenly felt that she had come home. For the first time in many months she felt safe and secure. Luke loved her! Although he hadn't said in so many words she was quite sure he did, and she loved him. But you once thought you loved Mark, an inner voice seemed to say. How can you be sure this time? It was true. How could she be certain that on this occasion it would be a lasting love? If Luke hurt her as Mark had done would she so easily turn to someone else? Was she incapable of ever truly loving one man for the rest of her life?

Luke's next words were as though he knew what was on her mind. 'I love you, Taryn. I've wanted to tell you for so long, but I haven't dared. I was never quite sure where I stood with you.'

She lifted her head and smiled and their lips met in a mutually satisfying kiss before Taryn remembered where they were and struggled to free herself. 'Your mother——' she began.

'My mother,' he repeated, 'knows exactly how I feel.'

'You mean you told her—before me?'

'I had to tell someone, and I have no secrets from Helen. She's the most wonderful mother a guy could ask for and since my father died she's turned to me more and more. Don't get me wrong, she's not the possessive type. Her ambition is to see me happily married,' and then anxiously, 'You do like her?'

Taryn nodded and smiled. 'It would be impossible not to, and I'm sure she'll get on fine with Gammy.'

'So,' said Luke, leading her over to the settee, 'that brings us back to you and me. Now you know how I feel—and that I've not got a wife tucked away some-where—dare I ask whether you return my love?'

Taryn looked at him for a long minute. She wanted to say yes, but how could she be sure? 'I—I think so,' she said at last. 'I mean, yes, of course I do.'

He touched her cheek gently. 'You don't sound very certain.'

'When I thought you had a wife I was crazy with jealousy. I'd made up my mind to go away, never to see you again. When you invited us to lunch I wanted to refuse. I didn't want to meet her. Oh, Luke, does that answer your question?'

His answer was to draw her close and rain kisses on her face. 'Darling Taryn, how you've suffered—and so unnecessarily. But no more. How soon will you marry me?'

This question was so unexpected that Taryn drew back in surprise. 'Give me time,' she husked. 'I'm not yet used to the fact that you love me.'

'Surely it's sufficient that I do? And if you feel the same there's no reason to wait.' His dark eyes pleaded with her.

'Luke, please don't rush me. I will marry you, but I don't feel ready for it yet.'

Taryn was not prepared for the angry frown which replaced his good humour. 'I might have known,' he grated. 'It's Mark, isn't it? Won't you *ever* forget him? Am I to live with his memory for the rest of my life?'

'Please,' she protested, 'I'm doing my best, but it's impossible to completely forget someone you once thought you loved.'

'I think you still love him,' Luke stated matter-of-factly, looking suddenly tired and dispirited.

'I don't. He killed what love I had for him when he told me about Maria.'

'Do you mean to tell me,' he said quietly, 'that if Mark walked into this room right now you would have no feelings for him whatsoever?'

It was a difficult question and Taryn was silent for so long that Luke gave a snort of disgust and springing to his feet crossed over to the window. He pushed his hands into his pockets and stared out across the valley. Taryn made a tentative gesture towards him, but knew that unless she could give him a positive answer he would only rebuff her. Yet how could she? How did she know what her reaction would be?

'Please, Luke,' she said at length. 'It's an impossible question and as the matter is unlikely to arise I see no point in trying to give you an answer.'

'Is it so unlikely?' He swung round to face her. 'Stranger things have happened.'

Taryn shrugged. 'If you feel like that there's no point in going on. I can't say how I'd react. I could tell you now, in all honesty, that if we did meet he would mean nothing to me at all. On the other hand,

I might find I'm still in love with him.'

'So how long have I to wait until you make up your mind?'

'Perhaps—a Christmas wedding would be nice,' suggested Taryn hesitantly. 'That would give me time to——'

'Christmas!' he interrupted harshly. 'Six months! Damn you, woman, I want you now. I won't wait that long.' He strode forward and pulled her roughly into his arms. She was aware of a throbbing passion as he kissed her—a harsh, punishing kiss—a demanding kiss. 'I'll give you three weeks,' he said thickly. 'If you can't give me your answer by then you can forget I ever asked you.'

CHAPTER SEVEN

TARYN was alone in the room when her aunt returned. After that brutal kiss Luke had stormed out and Taryn, on the verge of tears, had curled up in a chair desperately trying to straighten her muddled thoughts. Of course she wanted to marry Luke. She loved him, so why hesitate? The chances of Mark ever coming to England, to Ferndale at least, were so remote it was laughable. What doubts she had would soon disperse once she became Luke's wife.

'Taryn love, what's the matter?' Her aunt came straight to her side. 'Where's Luke? You haven't quarrelled?'

Taryn shook her head. 'A slight difference of opinion, that's all. It will pass.'

'It looks more than that to me,' observed Gammy drily. 'What have you been saying?'

'What have I said? Really, Gammy, don't you think it could be Luke who's at fault?'

'I doubt it.'

'If you must know,' realising that her aunt would ferret out the information one way or another, 'Luke's asked me to marry him.'

Her aunt's face lit up before frowning anxiously. 'You've accepted, of course?'

'Not exactly. I told him I wasn't sure.'

'But you love him.'

'I know, but I'm afraid. I once thought I loved Mark. What if it happens all over again?'

'Now you're being foolish.' Gammy drew up a footstool and sat beside the young girl. 'Everyone has a first love, whether it's a schoolteacher, a pop star, or the first man they date; but just because it doesn't turn out it doesn't mean the same will happen with the next man. It's a risk we all have to take. Only you know how you feel. If you love him enough —and I think you do—then go ahead and marry him. Otherwise you'll regret it for the rest of your life.'

Taryn drew a deep breath and expelled it slowly. 'I wanted to wait until Christmas, but Luke won't. He's given me three weeks, and after that it will be all over between us.'

Gammy regarded her niece gravely. 'I've never told you before,' she said, 'but I met and married your Uncle James within a month and neither of us ever regretted it. My only sorrow now is that he's not alive to see his great-grandson. If I were you I'd think again about asking him to wait. I've felt all along that you were right for each other; it would be a pity to lose him because you took too long to make up your mind.'

'I suppose you're right,' admitted Taryn, 'but I haven't the nerve to tell him now. I'll wait until the three weeks are up. At least it will give me more time to get used to the idea.'

'As you wish.' Gammy rose and stood looking down at Taryn. 'I must say it was a pleasant surprise to find out that Helen was Luke's mother. However did you manage to get the wrong impression?'

Taryn lifted her shoulders dispassionately. 'Andy called her Mrs Major—I assumed the rest.'

'And suffered sleepless nights because of it? Never mind, love, it looks as though all will turn out well in the end.'

Taryn nodded grimly. 'Let's hope so,' and then with an effort to appear more cheerful, 'Does Helen need any help in the kitchen?'

Gammy shook her head. 'She turned me out; says she works best alone, but it shouldn't be long. Shall we go into the dining room?'

The rosewood table set with sparkling silver and snowy white linen was enhanced by an arrangement of wild roses, arranged so artistically that they could not have looked better had they been the most expensive of blooms. It added the finishing touch to an otherwise austere room with its regency-striped curtains and matching upholstered chairs. The sculptured carpet in palest beige muffled their steps and Luke, standing near the window, did not hear them enter. When Gammy spoke he looked round and Taryn caught a brief look of anguish on his face before he made a visible effort to control his feelings.

'Lunch is ready if you'd like to sit down,' he said. 'I'll help Helen bring it in.'

Taryn caught his hand as he brushed past her, unable to bear the thought that she was the cause of his grief. 'I'm sorry,' she whispered, 'I didn't think you'd——'

'Forget it,' he cut in with a sidelong glance at Gammy.

The older woman took the opportunity of saying:

'If it will be of any help, young man, I'm on your side. I'm glad you've given her an ultimatum, but make sure you stick to it.'

'I intend to,' he said grimly before carrying on out of the room.

Taryn wished her aunt had said nothing, or at least waited until she was alone with Luke. They sat on in silence, each full of their own thoughts, until Luke reappeared wheeling the dinner trolley, Helen following with a bottle of champagne.

'I thought we'd celebrate our first party in the new house,' she smiled. 'Unless you can think of anything better?' looking expectantly from Luke to Taryn. Taryn guessed what was on her mind and shook her head quickly.

'I think it's a splendid idea. It's such a beautiful place. I'm so glad it's going to be lived in again after all these years.'

Luke uncorked the bottle and their luncheon began with much merriment. For the moment at least Luke appeared to have forgotten his earlier upset and did his best to entertain their guests.

Home-made vegetable soup was followed by a beef casserole marinated in a red wine and cooked with button onions, mushrooms and carrots. It was delicious, and Taryn ate so well she was forced to refuse the cream caramel that came afterwards. It was altogether a very satisfying meal and by the time they had finished Taryn had almost suppressed all thoughts of her disagreement with Luke. He treated her no differently, and had Taryn not guessed that this was a front put on for his mother's benefit she might have decided that he had forgiven her earlier indecision.

They were drinking their coffee in the lounge when Gammy brought up the subject of Mark. 'Has Luke told you he's got a double?' she remarked casually to Helen.

Taryn glanced across at Helen and caught the swift look of—was it horror?—in her eyes before she smiled blandly and said, 'Really? How interesting,' and turning to her son, 'You never said. Have you met this—er—supposed double of yours?'

Luke, who had been standing behind his mother and had not seen her reaction to Gammy's unexpected question, shook his head. 'He's a friend of Taryn's, not mine. You'd better ask her.'

Still trying to puzzle out why Helen Major should have reacted so strangely, Taryn nodded and smiled. 'I met him in Italy. The first time I saw Luke I thought it was him. In fact it took me ages to convince myself that he was not Mark.'

'Mark?' Her voice had grown faint and she put a hand to her breast.

'Are you all right, Helen?' Taryn looked up at Luke, a swift frown creasing her brow.

Swiftly Luke bent over his mother. 'Helen!' he said urgently. 'Where are your tablets?'

'My bag,' she mouthed, her face now devoid of colour.

He was out of the room in two strides and almost before they had time to speak was back with a glass of water and the bottle of tablets. Shaking two into his hand, he put one arm round Helen's shoulders and steadied the glass as she swallowed.

'It's her heart,' he explained to a worried Gammy and Taryn. 'One of the reasons I wanted to bring her out here. She's been so much better this last couple of days, but I suppose she's overdone it today.'

'I wish we'd known,' Gammy responded. 'We wouldn't have come.'

'Precisely. That's why I didn't tell you. Helen wanted you here. Don't worry, she'll be all right in a minute.' And as if in answer to his words the colour returned to Helen's cheeks and she gave her guests a wan smile.

But Taryn knew that it was not the extra work that had caused this sudden attack. It was something to do with Mark and Luke. All along she had felt there was some connection—and Helen knew what it was! In that case had Luke been lying when he professed not to know Mark Vandyke? Did he in fact know him—or, to be precise, was he Mark? The scar which she had considered definite proof of Mark's identity could have been removed by plastic surgery. Once again she was faced with the thought that Luke was Mark but for some reason he did not want her to know.

As Luke himself did not seem to realise that his mother's spasm was caused by mention of Mark, Taryn decided there was no point in continuing the conversation—in any case, due to his mother's condition—it would be wise never to mention Mark again.

'I'm so sorry,' Helen made an effort to speak. 'Please forgive me. I——'

Gammy held up her hand. 'Don't try to apologise. I think you ought to be in bed—Luke?' looking at him. 'You take her. Taryn and I will clear away and wash up.'

They decided to go soon after that, but Taryn was disappointed when Luke did not try to persuade them to stay, fully aware that it was not entirely due to his mother's condition.

Back at the cottage she said very little and Gammy made no attempt to draw her into conversation. Taryn wondered whether her aunt had noticed Helen's reaction to her observations about Mark or whether she was of the same opinion as Luke in that it was the extra work that had caused his mother's upset. She had no desire to bring up the topic herself as she was sure Gammy would only declare that she was imagining things. As with Luke her aunt thought she was making too much of this resemblance between the two men. They would never understand how important it was to her to discover the truth, both with regard to her own feelings and the positive identity of Luke.

She took Dainty out for another ride later on, but even this did not help. Usually a gallop over the moors was the solution to all her problems, but on this occasion, it appeared, it would take more than fresh air and a clear head to put her thoughts into order.

Monday and Tuesday passed with no sign of Luke. Taryn wondered whether he was going to leave her alone for the entire three weeks when on Wednesday morning the doorbell rang as they were having breakfast. She answered the door and met Luke's rugged smile. Her relief must have been evident, for he laughed. 'Did you think I'd forgotten you? I've been chasing round trying to fix my mother up with some staff.'

'How is she?' asked Taryn at once, knowing that she ought to have gone up to Dale End and inquired, but a reticence to face Luke had held her back. Since Sunday she had built up a mental picture of him as an impostor, but looking at him now, with his open, honest face, and those tawny eyes smiling into her own, she felt her decision wavering. Luke would never lie—he loved her; he wanted to marry her. She smiled back, her fears evaporating beneath the warmth of his regard.

'She's fine. Still insists on doing too much, but now that I've managed to find a housekeeper she can relax and I can leave her without worrying that she's going to over-exert herself again.'

Taryn realised that she had kept him standing on the doorstep as though he were a stranger, and she stepped back. 'Come on in. We're just having breakfast.'

The door closed behind him, but before they reached the kitchen he pulled her swiftly into his arms. 'I've been waiting to do this,' he said, his kisses devouring her face. 'I've missed you, Taryn. Oh, God, how I've missed you!'

Taryn poised on tiptoe, her arms round his neck, and returned his kisses passionately. Here in his arms all thoughts of the other man fled. She increased the pressure on her hands and pulled his head closer. Her lips parted beneath the urgency of his kiss. She felt the strong beat of his heart increasing in pace with his growing need of her. In that moment there was no doubt in her mind. She loved him completely and irrevocably. Should she give him her answer now or wait until the three weeks were up?

'Who is it, Taryn?' Gammy's voice from the kitchen broke into her thoughts. The moment was gone.

Luke pushed her away with a wry grin. 'We'll continue later—when we're unlikely to be disturbed.'

Taryn's stomach muscles tightened at the thought of such delights and she smiled shyly before smoothing down her hair and leading him into the kitchen.

They spent the day on the moors. Gammy packed a picnic lunch, the sun shone out of a cloudless sky, and altogether Taryn could not have asked for a better day. Luke did not mention marriage again, so Taryn followed suit and concentrated on enjoying his delightful company. He seemed intent on making her happy and by the time they reached home again Taryn had been lulled into a false sense of security, little knowing that in less than an hour her whole new world was to be suddenly disrupted.

Gammy was out and Luke refused her invitation to coffee, expressing a desire to ensure his mother's comfort. So she made herself a drink and sat in the twilight musing over the day's events. Their tramp across the moors had left her feeling hot and dusty and she intended taking a bath later, but now the door bell shrilled into her silence. Musing whether it was

Luke or Gammy, having forgotten her key, she smiled softly to herself as she opened the door. 'Luke!' she exclaimed in delight. 'I guessed it might be you. How is your mother?'

The semi-darkness threw his features into shadow and she could not see his response, but she felt the sudden frown and the tensing of his limbs as he took a step forward. 'Taryn, are you crazy or something?'

It was as she stepped back into the room that a chilling fear clutched at Taryn's heart. She snapped on the light and took a closer look at the man who had spoken. At the impeccable silver grey mohair suit, the white silk shirt, relieved only by an emerald tie and matching handkerchief protruding from the breast pocket. At his face——amber eyes regarding her closely, brown hair swept into the familiar wave across his brow, full lips, now compressed.

Luke had been wearing brown slacks and a beige shirt and it seemed unlikely that he would go to the extent of dressing in such a manner at this hour. It could only be one other person. Her hand flew involuntarily to her throat, her mouth felt suddenly dry and when she opened her lips no sound came.

Then he was shaking her gently by the shoulders. 'Taryn, what's the matter? I know it must be a surprise me turning up here like this, but ——'

His voice was fading. Taryn felt suddenly light-headed, her heart beat at an alarming rate. After that she knew nothing until she opened her eyes to find herself lying on the settee. Mark was kneeling at her side, a glass of water in his hand, imploring her to drink.

He had never been any good in an emergency and Taryn could see that he was shaken by her reaction. She allowed him to slip an arm about her shoulders and lift her sufficiently to sip the welcome liquid. Her mouth still felt parched and her head ached. She lay back and closed her eyes. It was all a dream—when she woke he would be gone.

But he was not.

He stood looking down at her, a worried frown creasing his brow. Taryn realised that since their first greeting she had not spoken. Incredibility had robbed her of speech. But now with the returning of her senses came also the recollection of their last meeting. Surprising strength returned to her body. She swung her legs to the floor and pushed herself up, swaying for a moment before regaining her equilibrium. Mark put out a hand to steady her, but she backed away, eyeing him warily and not a little angrily. 'What are you doing here?' she rasped. 'In case you've forgotten, I said I never wanted to see you again.'

'I know,' he said quietly, his voice controlled and even, despite the tell-tale muscle that jerked spasmodically in his jaw. 'Things have changed. I wanted to——'

'I bet they have,' cut in Taryn harshly. 'You've no need to tell me, I can guess. But if you think you can come crawling back to me, you're mistaken.' She lifted her arm and pointed. 'The door's that way.'

The man shook his head. 'Please listen. It's not what you think. I need you, Taryn.'

'Spare me the sob stuff,' she said impatiently, turning away and folding her arms in a resigned gesture. 'How did you find me, anyway? I don't recall giving you my address.'

'No, but you've mentioned Ferndale so many times it was a matter of simple deduction to track you down. Once I'd found the village I only had to ask.'

Taryn glanced at him sharply. 'Who told you?'

He shrugged lightly. 'Does it matter? Some young woman with a pram. Though I must confess she looked at me very strangely. Would it have anything to do with the fact that you called me Luke?'

Janice's mind must be boggling, decided Taryn with wry amusement—probably the whole village knew by now that Mark had turned up. As far as her own feelings were concerned she still felt too numbed to really grasp the situation. Only one thing stood out above everything else—Luke had been telling her the truth after all. Realising he was still waiting for her answer, she slowly nodded. 'I've met—someone else —who looks like you.'

'So what? Many people look alike.'

'Yes, but when I say he looks like you I mean exactly that. He's your double. In fact when we first met I thought he was you.'

'As you thought I was him?' He stroked his chin reflectively. 'Amazing, though I suppose most people have doubles—it's just that they never meet.'

'I don't see how you can dismiss it so lightly. It's uncanny, the likeness between you—but I'll tell you one thing, he would never do the dirty on me. He's more of a gentleman than you.'

Mark had the graciousness to look abashed. 'I'm sorry,' he said softly. 'But it was no use going through with it when I—I'd met someone else who I loved more.'

'And what's happened now?' sneered Taryn. 'Have you tired of her as well?'

Mark's face clouded. He seemed to have difficulty in choosing the right words. His voice when he did speak was barely audible. 'Maria's dead!'

Taryn stared at him, momentarily stunned by this revelation, then she touched his arm. 'Oh, Mark, I'm so sorry. Why did you let me go on like that?'

He shook his head, apparently fighting an emotion that was stronger than him. Taryn felt a lump in her throat and the prick of tears behind her eyes. It was the first time she had seen a man so near to breaking down. Involuntarily she stepped closer, her only thoughts that somehow she must console him.

When his arms crushed her relentlessly to him Taryn knew it was not passion that made him act this way, merely a desire to be comforted as she had turned to Gammy in her time of distress. 'Taryn,' he murmured brokenly. 'There was no one else who would understand. I had to come and see you.'

'I know, I know,' she soothed, pushing her fingers through the thickness of his hair and pulling his head closer to hers. Mark had no family to whom he could turn and she knew he was too proud to let his colleagues see his pain. She was surprised that he had sought her out, but pleased too—so long as he did not think he could carry on where he left off. All that was over now. In one respect this coming of Mark was a blessing, for she now knew without a shadow of doubt that she no longer loved him. No response flared up inside her at his touch. The fires that had burned were finally put out. Luke was the only man for her.

As her thoughts ran along these lines the door opened and over Mark's shoulder Taryn saw Luke's smiling face. 'Surprise, sur——' he began, stopping abruptly when he saw her in the arms of another man, his face darkening in an angry flush. Without giving her time to speak he disappeared, slamming the door behind him.

Taryn struggled to free herself and fled to the door. 'Luke,' she called, 'please come back, I can explain!' But he was already striding up the hill and gave no indication that he had heard her plaintive cry.

She was on the point of running after him when Mark appeared at her side, an inquiring lift to his eyebrows. 'What was that all about?'

Taryn rounded on him crossly. 'Now look what you've done! That was Luke. He thinks that you and I were——' She ran her fingers wearily through her hair. 'Oh, hell,' her voice quieter now, 'what a mess!' It wasn't Mark's fault. It was unfair to blame him, but all the same she could not help resenting his presence. From the look on Luke's face he would never believe that there was a perfectly simple explanation to her actions.

Mark took her arm and led her back inside. 'Pity he went like that; I should like to have met him.' He had regained his composure by now and threw himself down on one of the armchairs, studying her harassed face with apparent unconcern. 'Do you love this man?'

Taryn nodded. 'He's asked me to marry him.'

Mark's brows shot up. 'Then it looks as though I've come just in time.'

'What do you mean?'

'Isn't it obvious? You can't marry him now—it's me you love, remember? "I'll love you for ever," you used to say.'

'Did I?' asked Taryn haughtily. 'Then you have only yourself to blame. If you hadn't treated me as though I were of no consequence perhaps I should still love you. As it is—I love Luke.'

'That's only because he reminds you of me. Once you get used to the idea that I still love you, and want you to become my wife, you'll realise that it's me you love after all.'

How conceited he sounded, thought Taryn. How had she ever thought that he and Luke were alike? In looks, maybe, but in temperament—no. 'Is that your real reason for coming here?' she blazed. 'Not for consolation but because you thought I'd be ready to carry on as though nothing had happened?' What a fool she had been in offering her sympathy. He had known exactly what he was doing and if Luke had not walked in at that moment goodness knows what might have happened.

'Is it such a bad reason?' he asked. 'We got on well together, you and me, I don't see why we shouldn't continue that way.'

'You mean we used to. Don't you understand—it's

143

all over now. I want nothing more to do with you.'
She crossed to the window and looked out at the
darkening sky, her shoulders stiff with resentment.

Mark came to stand close behind her. 'You can't
really mean that?' His voice was low and persuasive.
'After all that's gone between us, doesn't it mean
anything to you?'

Taryn took a deep breath. 'Did it to you, when
you married Maria?' she asked bitterly.

'Now you're being unfair. I explained to you how
I felt then.'

'Don't you think it might work both ways?'

'You don't mean that you love Luke more than
you do me?'

He sounded incredulous and Taryn stifled a laugh.
'That's right—I'm sorry you've had a wasted journey.
You should have let me know so I could have put
you in the picture.'

She heard his swift indrawn breath and the next
second his hands were on her shoulders, whipping
her round to face him. 'Give me a chance,' he said.
'Don't turn me away without letting me try to prove
that it's not all over between us.'

His fingers bit into the soft flesh of her upper
arms, causing her to wince and try to free herself.
'What's the use? You mean nothing to me now, do
you hear? Nothing!'

'I refuse to give in without a fight. Besides,' suddenly letting her go, 'I want to see this twin soul of
mine who has succeeded in persuading my girl that
she loves him.'

Taryn glared. 'For the last time, I am *not* your

girl!' Then resignedly, 'If you want to stay around that's up to you—but you'll be wasting your time.'

Gammy chose that moment to return. She smiled at her niece and the man standing beside her. 'Hello, Taryn, Luke. Had a good day?'

'It's not Luke,' returned Taryn, stiff-lipped. 'It's Mark.'

Her aunt's smile faded and she took a closer look at her niece's companion. 'Really?' She shook her head. 'I never altogether believed you when you said they were so alike,' she admitted. 'Now I see why you were so shocked.'

'Forgive my intrusion.' Mark turned a winning smile on the older woman. 'I see you've heard all about me; no doubt you're wondering why I'm here?'

Gammy inclined her head. 'Something of the sort did cross my mind.'

'Perhaps Taryn would like to tell you,' he said pleasantly, looking obliquely at his former fiancée.

'His wife's died,' said Taryn bluntly. If he thought she was going to be tactful he could think again. The time had passed when she cared whether or not she hurt his feelings. 'So he's come to see if I'd care to take her place.'

'Oh, I am sorry,' said Gammy instantly. 'What happened? You must forgive my niece,' with a warning glance in Taryn's direction, 'but you did hurt her.'

'A car accident. It was my fault, I was driving too fast. Luckily I was thrown clear and received only superficial injuries.' He showed none of the emotion that he had displayed in front of Taryn. He

145

was either keeping himself under tight control, decided the younger girl, or else he had put on a very good act for her benefit. Her lips tightened. The latter thought suggested itself as being the most likely.

'I see.' Gammy studied his face. 'Has Taryn told you about Luke?'

He nodded. 'Yes, but of course there's no question of her carrying on with him now. I mean, she's always loved me. She took up with him on the rebound. I know I didn't treat her fairly, but—well, that's all in the past. From now on——'

'Not so fast, young man.' Gammy held up her hand. 'It's not so simple as that. Perhaps she did love you, perhaps she still does; only Taryn can give us the answer, but Luke is not a person to be dismissed lightly. He's a very fine man and I would welcome him as a husband for my great-niece. I don't know anything about you—except that you're a fashion designer—and I would certainly want to know a lot more before I allowed Taryn to marry you. You've let her down once, how are we to know it wouldn't happen again?'

'Don't worry, Gammy, I'm not going to marry him,' pronounced Taryn. 'I was on the point of turning him out when you came.'

'And I was going to ask if you knew anywhere I could stay for the night,' interposed Mark. 'I don't recall seeing any hotels in this godforsaken place.'

'Perhaps it's not quite what you're used to,' offered Gammy with a slight lift of her brows, 'but we like it. You've left it a little late to try and find accommodation now. You'd best stay here the night.'

'Gammy!' exclaimed Taryn in undisguised horror.

Her aunt continued as though she had not spoken. 'Of course the camp bed's not very comfortable and you'll have to be up early as we use this room for our meals, but you're quite welcome.'

Mark's face was a picture when he realised he would be expected to sleep on a makeshift bed in the living room. It would be fun, decided Taryn, to see how he adapted himself—if indeed he accepted the invitation.

'I suppose I have no alternative,' he said ungraciously, 'though I'm sure I shan't sleep a wink. Don't you have a spare room?'

'Sorry,' smiled Taryn. 'We only boast two bedrooms. We live very modestly, as you can see.'

'Indeed I do,' drily. 'I suppose you do have a bathroom—or is that another of the amenities I'm going to have to do without?'

'Oh yes, we're not completely uncivilised. Would you like a cup of coffee?'

'I'd prefer a Scotch—or is that asking too much?'

'Afraid so. I can offer you a glass of sherry?' knowing full well he detested that particular drink.

'No, thanks, I'll take the coffee, strong and black with no sugar.'

'I hadn't forgotten,' returned Taryn tartly, relieved to be able to escape into the kitchen.

Her aunt followed a few seconds later. 'He's gone to fetch his case,' she stated in response to Taryn's questioning look. 'Tell me, were you really in love with him? I'm not very impressed. He doesn't seem your type at all.'

'I thought I was.' Taryn stared reflectively at the kettle in her hand. 'He seems different now.'

'Since you met Luke, you mean? Luke is so much more of a man, don't you think, yet he's not proud. I bet Mark's never roughed it before.'

Taryn was forced to laugh. 'You guessed that when you asked him. I'm surprised he agreed.'

'If it wasn't for you I doubt if he would. He'd have been away to Exeter or Plymouth to one of the best hotels.'

'I wish he would,' said Taryn, spooning coffee fiercely into the cups. 'I wish he'd never come. Everything was going so well. I nearly told Luke today that I'd marry him. I wish I had. Now everything's ruined.'

'Not necessarily. Perhaps in the morning you'll be able to persuade Mark that it's Luke you love and he'll go away before Luke even knows he's been here.'

'It's too late.' Taryn faced her aunt sadly, her eyes like two haunted pools in her pale, taut face. 'Luke's already seen him—with me in his arms. He didn't even wait for an explanation. It's all over now. He'll never believe there's nothing between us any more. I've lost him, Gammy.' Two tears rolled slowly down her cheeks and fell on to the table. 'What am I going to do?'

CHAPTER EIGHT

GAMMY looked in concern at her niece's bowed head. 'Of one thing I'm sure,' she said. 'You're not going to give in without a fight. Go up there, tell Luke exactly what happened; tell him you love him and want to marry him. He's a fair man. Once he's had time to cool down he'll listen to you.'

'I wish I had your conviction,' sighed Taryn.

'It's the only way. How else will he find out the truth? Never let pride stand between you and the man you love, Taryn. It can be your worst enemy. First thing after breakfast up you go to Dale End and make him listen.'

As Taryn lay in bed that night she recalled Gammy's words. Her aunt was right as usual. It would be stupid to let Luke go on thinking she loved another man for the sake of her pride. It would be a hard task—she never easily humbled herself before anyone—but if she wanted Luke, and she did, there was no other way. It was unlikely he would make the first move himself. He had seen what he thought was a passionate embrace between her and another man —he wouldn't know it was Mark. Perhaps when she explained that she had been consoling him over the death of his wife he would realise that he had made a mistake. She would tell him then that she wanted to marry him—and the sooner the better.

Although Taryn was tired after her long day out sleep was elusive. Thoughts of her coming meeting with Luke prevented her from relaxing. And the man downstairs. Why hadn't he written instead of turning up like this? She could have then explained that she wanted nothing more to do with him, that all the love she had ever felt had been killed the day he told her he was going to marry Maria. But of course he couldn't! He had not known her address. If only he had found some way, though, of contacting her beforehand none of this would have happened.

The grey fingers of dawn were creeping slowly across the sky before she fell into a fitful sleep. The sound of running water and a man's voice singing in the bathroom woke her up. Immediately her mind returned to the previous night. Thoughts of the task in front of her made her curl back down between the sheets reluctant to face the new day, but when she heard Mark go downstairs she realised there was no point in delaying. If she wanted any happiness at all Luke had to be faced—and the sooner the better.

After much deliberation she decided to wear an Italian silk dress in shades of blues and mauves. It was one she had brought back from Naples but which like most of her other clothes had been discarded for shirts and slacks since returning to England. The softly clinging material enhanced her curves and she knew she looked her best. She needed to—as an armour in which to face Luke. With a hint of blue shadow on her eyelids and the merest trace of lipstick she felt more confident and there was an almost jaunty air to her feet as she descended into the living room.

She could hear her aunt preparing breakfast in the kitchen, but Mark was lolling in an armchair, one leg strung over the side and a cigarette hanging indolently between his fingers. He wore sky blue suede trousers and a silk shirt in the same shade, looking entirely out of place in the homely atmosphere of chintz and brass. 'Good morning, darling,' he greeted her brightly. 'Is that dress in my honour?'

Taryn had completely forgotten that it had once been one of his favourites. She felt like tearing it off and dragging herself into denim jeans -which would be completely abhorrent to Mark's fastidious nature. She tried to look disdainful. 'Why should I dress for you? If you must know I'm going to see Luke this morning—to apologise for yesterday.'

'Why should you do that? If he wants to put his own interpretation on what we were doing, then let him.'

'To leave you a clear field?' retorted Taryn hotly, 'No, thank you. I love Luke and I don't intend losing him,' and with a deliberate change of subject, 'Did you have a good night?'

He took a long pull on his cigarette and slowly expelled the smoke into the air. 'You're hoping I'll say no. It would amuse you tremendously to think I'd lain awake all night. As a matter of fact I slept very well--due no doubt to the fact that I'd been travelling all day and was rather tired—but all the same I slept soundly and didn't wake until your good lady aunt came rattling through with the vacuum cleaner.'

Taryn hid a smile. Gammy was not usually so inconsiderate, but it was clear she had taken a dislike to Mark and was doing all she could to discourage him from staying another night. 'I'll go and see if she needs any help with the breakfast.'

Mark made no attempt to join them, and Taryn thought that here again was proof of the difference between the two men. Luke would have soon offered his assistance; indeed he would have insisted on doing his share.

'What are your plans now, Mark?' asked Gammy as soon as breakfast was over. 'Will you be returning to Italy?'

'I don't think so.' Mark studied his nails as though they were of paramount importance. 'I think I'll hang around for a little while longer, to give Taryn a chance to make up her mind.'

'You've got a nerve!' flashed Taryn indignantly. 'Don't you ever listen to anything I say?'

'I don't believe you've changed so much,' he said smoothly. 'What's happened to the Taryn who was so grateful I'd noticed her that she professed undying love?'

'Don't start that again. Let's say I didn't know my own mind. The romance of a new job in a new country, coupled with your attentions turned my head. It's over now—finished—and I don't want to discuss it any more.'

'So, young man,' intervened Gammy, 'now you know where you stand there's no point in staying.

Tayrn won't change her mind.'

He smiled, completely unperturbed by Gammy's outspokenness. 'All the same, I think I'll spend a few more days here. Of course, I won't put on you any more—charming though your hospitality is—I'll find a good hotel. There must surely be some around here somewhere?'

'In any of the larger towns,' Gammy answered drily, 'though don't forget it's the holiday season.'

Half an hour later Taryn was ready to leave. Mark had so far shown no signs of moving, so she held out her hand. 'This is goodbye, then. No doubt you'll be gone when I return. I can't say I'm sorry things haven't turned out the way you wanted, but I am sorry about Maria, truly.'

He held her hand slightly longer than was necessary. 'I think I'll wait. You never know—Luke may not believe you, then you'll be glad of a shoulder to cry on. Sure you wouldn't like me to come with you? I'd still like to meet him.'

'No, thanks,' replied Taryn distantly, 'and I fear you'll be wasting your time. Even if——' her voice shook, 'if Luke doesn't believe me, I shan't come back to you.'

'We'll see,' he smiled—so confidently that Taryn felt like shaking him.

She decided against taking the car. The path up to Dale End was now worn clear enough for her to walk without difficulty and the few extra minutes would allow her time to rehearse her explanation. But instead Mark's smile still lingered in her mind's eye. He was arrogant, so conceited. He couldn't bear to think that any woman would reject his advances. Not for the first time Taryn wondered how she had ever fallen in love with him.

Upon reaching the door she hesitated, her hand on the lion's head knocker, which she noticed irrelevantly had been given a fresh coat of black paint. Then with a determined gesture she allowed it to fall from her hand, closing her eyes at the vibrant sound that seemed to echo throughout the house.

The door opened immediately, almost as though she had been expected. Taryn encountered Luke's cold disapproval and flinched reflexively. He stood back for her to enter and she shivered despite the warmth of the day. He took no pains to hide his condemnation and as Taryn followed him to his study she felt reproval in every line of his back. She wanted to turn and run, but the thought of Mark waiting—expecting her to fail—increased her resolution to convince Luke that he was mistaken.

Once in his study he turned to face her. Still he had not spoken and was clearly waiting for Taryn to make the first move. Her heart went cold at the stony look on his face. Where was the Luke she knew and loved? Where was the man who had asked her to marry him?

'I—I want to explain,' she began. 'It wasn't what you thought. Mark was upset—I was comforting him.'

'Mark!' He said the name reflectively. 'I should have known. But that's a feeble excuse if ever there was one. I think I prefer to put my own interpretation on what I saw.'

'But it's true.' Taryn took an unconscious step forward. 'You must believe me. Mark's wife died and he——'

'Decided to see if number one was willing to take her place—and you, of course, jumped at the proposition. Didn't I tell you that you'd run straight into his arms if he turned up here?' He paused a moment before continuing, 'It also confirms my suspicions that he was the reason why you wouldn't give me a straight answer.'

His face was hard and Taryn cringed beneath the contempt in his words. 'Please,' she implored, 'please, Luke, you've got it all wrong. I don't love Mark; that's one thing I have found out.'

His eyebrows lifted sceptically. 'You expect me to believe that—after he spent the night at the cottage and you turn up here dressed in all your finery?' His eyes flickered over the dress before looking at her again with such harsh censure that Taryn felt the prick of tears behind her eyes. She blinked rapidly. Such feminine weakness would get her nowhere in this particular instance. 'Don't pretend that you dressed up for my benefit,' he continued. 'Before today—your meeting with my mother excepted— you didn't consider me sufficiently important to wear a dress; despite my making it clear when we first met that I despise women in trousers. I suppose Mark's different. His opinion is all that matters now.'

Taryn stamped her foot. 'Why won't you listen? When you saw us Mark had just finished telling me about his wife. Naturally he was upset——'

'And naturally you went into his arms?'

'Purely out of sympathy. That's all there was to it.'

'Are you trying to say that Mark came all the way from Italy just to tell you his wife had died? Can you deny that he hasn't tried to persuade you to go back with him?' He looked through the window. The cottage was clearly visible—and Mark's car outside. 'Is he waiting now for your answer? Don't be afraid of hurting me, Taryn. I think I knew from the moment we met that Mark would always take first place in your life. I tried to make you forget him God knows how I tried—but it was like banging my head against a brick wall. Please go now. There's nothing more to be said.'

'No, I won't!' Taryn was shouting now. 'Not until you've heard the full story. When Mark turned up I thought it was you—then when I found out who he really was I told him to go. He asked me to listen —he told me about his wife's death—that was when you turned up. I told him I loved you, that you'd asked me to marry you.'

'So why didn't he go?'

Taryn averted her eyes. 'He refused to believe that I still didn't love him. He—he did ask me to become his wife, but I said no; I said that all the love I had ever had for him was gone, killed by his own selfish desires. In fact, I don't think I ever did truly love him—not in the same way——.' Her voice tailed off. Her outburst was having no visible effect on Luke. He still stood tall and impassive—and critical.

'The fact that he's not gone proves he still thinks there's a chance. You didn't do a very good job of convincing him—or me. Perhaps you want the best of both worlds. I've given up trying to understand you. All I know is that I'm not prepared to sit back and wait while you decide. You had your chance, Taryn. It's too late now. I wish you and Mark every happiness.'

A sob broke in Taryn's throat as he picked up a letter from his desk. It was all over. There was nothing more she could do. Blindly she groped for the door; stumbled her way along the corridor, failing to see his mother until she had almost bumped into her.

'I wondered what all the shouting was about,' said Helen mildly, then observing the tears now coursing rapidly down Taryn's cheeks, 'My dear child, what is the matter?'

'I can't explain,' whispered Taryn brokenly. 'You'd best ask Luke.'

'Indeed I will,' asserted Helen, 'but you're coming with me. I won't have him upsetting you like this.' She frowned. 'It's most out of character. He acted strangely last night too—came in and shut himself in his room without saying a word. He was awake most of the night, I heard him prowling about. Was that anything to do with your argument now?'

Taryn nodded and Helen grasped her wrist determinedly. 'Come along, we'll sort this out between us,' and on a softer note, 'Don't worry, I'm sure we can overcome what's troubling you both. No partnership is without its ups and downs.'

His mother entered without knocking. Luke sat at his desk, head bowed in his hands, and did not hear their entrance. Taryn's heart contracted. *She* had done this to him. From the laughing happy man of yesterday he had been broken in spirit if not in heart. She moved forward, her hand outstretched, but Helen held her back, shaking her head in silent negation.

'Luke!' called Helen softly though imperatively. 'What have you done to this child?'

He looked up then, his eyes dull and glazed. After a cursory glance at his mother they rested impassionately on Taryn's tear-stained face. 'So, you thought you'd enlist my mother's help?' he grated thickly. 'I didn't think you'd resort to tricks like that.'

Helen looked sharply at her son. 'How dare you speak like that to Taryn!'

His eyes moved across to the older woman. 'Has she told you why I'm annoyed?—No,' he changed his mind, 'not annoyed—hurt, disappointed, disillusioned maybe—but not anger. It goes too deep for that.'

'Will someone please tell me what this is all about?' Helen spread her arms in an expression of bewilderment and sank on to the nearest chair.

'Very well.' Luke placed his hands on the desk and pushed himself to his feet. Crossing to the window, he gazed down at the valley. At Mark's car guessed Taryn, wishing she had escaped before Helen saw her distress. 'You remember Gammy mentioning a friend of Taryn's?' Though he was speaking to his mother he did not turn round and consequently did not see her startled expression. But Taryn watched carefully, ready to stop the conversation should she show the slightest sign of distress.

'I remember,' said Helen, her voice carefully controlled so that by not the slightest tremor did she give away her innermost feelings. 'Wasn't he the one who looked like you?'

'That's right. Well, he's turned up. He's down at the cottage now.' His tones were clipped and terse and still he did not face the occupants of the room.

Helen glanced swiftly at Taryn, her blue eyes bright and penetrating. 'Were you once in love with this man?'

Taryn nodded, unable to trust her voice.

'And now he's here you can't choose between him and my son? Is that what Luke's trying to tell me?'

'Is it hell!' Luke spoke loudly and emphatically, at last swinging round. The hatred in his eyes caused Taryn to cry out unconsciously. 'She's still in love with him—always has been. If I hadn't seen them together with my own eyes I might have believed the tale she's been trying to spin me, but now she can have him—I want nothing more to do with her!'

'Is this true, Taryn?' Helen's face was pale, but she still seemed to be fully in control of herself.

'No, it's not. I really do love Luke, Helen, but I've given up trying to persuade him. He saw me in Mark's arms and as far as he's concerned that was an admission of infidelity.'

Luke had resumed his stance by the window and his mother was silent for so long that Taryn began to feel uncomfortable and wonder whether the other woman too disbelieved her remarks; though when Taryn looked at her closely it appeared that she was struggling with some inner emotion. Was she about to suffer another attack? she speculated in concern, when Helen suddenly spoke.

'I have something to tell you, Luke. You can listen too, Taryn, as you are the unwitting cause of my decision. I've lived with this secret so long, often dreading you would find out and hold it against me, that in one way it's a relief to tell you now. If you despise me for it—well, you're a grown man, well able to take care of yourself.'

Luke had spun round as she spoke, a swift frown knitting his brows together. 'What are you talking about? What secret is this? You've never kept anything from me before.'

'I know, I know.' Her voice was weary. 'Sit down and listen and try to understand that what I did was for the best.'

He perched on the edge of his desk, one leg swinging freely. While waiting for his mother to begin he took a cigarette from a leather box, lighted it and threw back his head to exhale the smoke.

Taryn's hands were clenched tightly in her lap as she too sat on a nearby chair, waiting apprehensively and wondering what his mother was about to divulge.

Helen cleared her throat. 'The first, and most difficult thing for me to tell you, Luke, is that you are—that I——' She stopped, her eyes pleading with him to understand. 'You are adopted,' she finished in a rush. 'I'm not your real mother—though I love you as dearly as if you were my own flesh and blood.'

Taryn saw the swift flicker of surprise in Luke's eyes before they softened into a smile. 'I can't say this is not a shock,' he said. 'In fact, I'm completely bewildered—but it makes no difference, Helen dear.'

He slid off the desk and went down on his knees before her. 'Did you really think it would? Is that why you've never told me? I love you, Helen, and you've given me all the love and affection a man could ever ask for. In spite of what you say, you're still Mother to me.'

Tears filled Helen's eyes and Taryn felt as though she was intruding. As Luke cradled his mother's head on his shoulder she rose and tiptoed towards the door. Her hand was on the knob when Mrs Major said, 'Wait, I haven't finished.'

Taryn turned slowly back into the room. Luke too got to his feet and they stood looking down at the frail figure before them.

'You were only a few weeks old when you came to us. Naturally I never met your real mother, but I believe she's still alive and I shall understand if you feel the necessity to try and find her. Of course, that will be up to you'—a pregnant pause—'and—Mark.'

A breathless hush filled the room for a few seconds. Taryn was the first to speak.

'Mark! What has he to do with it?'

'Haven't you guessed?' Helen looked tired but her eyes caught and held those of the man who had been a son to her all these years. 'Mark is your brother. You are twins.' After this profound statement she leaned back in her chair, her eyes closed.

Taryn glanced hastily at Luke, once again afraid that Helen might be suffering as a result of her confession. To have lived all these years keeping the secret from Luke, for ever fearful he might find out and turn against her; and more especially dreading the thought that the two men might one day meet—and wonder—and eventually discover their relationship, must have been agony, and all Taryn's sympathy was with the other woman.

'How do you know it is Mark?' Luke asked his mother. 'You have no proof. The fact that he looks like me may be just coincidence.'

She opened her eyes and slowly shook her head. 'Too much of one to have both the name and the looks. Your mother's name was Rachael, your father Jacob, though they were never married. She insisted on giving her babies biblical names also and expressed a wish that they were never changed. It was a chance in a million that Taryn should meet and fall in love with you both.'

'Why were we separated?' Luke still looked sceptical. 'Surely it would have been better for—for me and my—brother—to have been adopted by the same family.'

'I believe the adoption society tried, but no one wanted two babies; in the end they reluctantly decided to part you. I promised never to tell, and if Mark had not appeared on the scene I doubt if I ever would.' She looked at Taryn. 'I can't see how this will help you with your problem, but,' her eyes returning to Luke, 'it might change your feelings towards Mark and in so doing perhaps you will not be so hard on Taryn.'

Again there was silence in the room, each member occupied with their own thoughts. Taryn felt completely bemused. Why hadn't she known? Surely it was obvious by their appearance that the two men were related? Everyone had agreed how uncanny it was.

'I'd like to meet him.' Helen's voice broke into her thoughts. 'Will you fetch him up here, Taryn?'

'Er—yes, of course, if Luke has no objection.' Judging by the look on his face he protested very strongly, and Taryn understood how he felt. If she herself had not been involved he might enjoy a new-found brother; as it was ...

Helen brushed aside her indecision. 'Luke has no say in the matter. Please, Taryn, go now.'

Afraid to look again at Luke, Taryn left the room and was soon retracing her steps to Honeysuckle Cottage. Little had she realised when she made the journey a short time earlier how events would turn out. It was incredible, like something out of a film or a novel. Things like this did not happen in real life. Yet it had. Though as his mother had said, how would it help their problem? Luke was still not convinced that she loved him and there was less likelihood of Mark leaving now and allowing them to reconcile their affairs.

Mark had been watching for her return and now he came out of the cottage, a confident smile on his lips. 'It's taken you long enough,' he accused. 'What's the verdict?'

'Luke's mother wants to see you,' stated Taryn flatly.

'His *mother*?' incredulously. 'What's going on? Surely he doesn't need her to fight his battles?'

'It's nothing like that. Come on. You'll find out when you get there. Prepare yourself for a shock, that's all.'

'Say, what is this? I'm not sure I want to go.' He twisted her round to face him. 'What have you been saying about me?'

'Please, Mark.' Taryn struggled to escape. 'There's no need to worry, but I feel that Mrs Major should tell you herself.'

Still looking suspicious, he let her go and together they climbed the hill. 'At least I'm getting my wish to meet Luke,' he jested, catching her arm as she stumbled over a hidden stone. 'By the way, you never said whether he'd forgiven me or if he still thinks that you and I are—er—lovers?'

'No, I didn't,' replied Taryn lightly, but still she did not give him the answer he wanted. It was a subject she did not wish to discuss; at least not for the time being.

As they neared Dale End Taryn observed Luke looking down from the window of his study. What was *he* feeling? Did he relish the idea of accepting Mark as his brother? conceived in the same womb yet parted almost at birth never to meet again for over thirty years. It must be a traumatic experience—for Mark too—once he discovered the presence of a twin.

Helen opened the door, one hand resting against the jamb as she studied the man at Taryn's side. He suffered her scrutiny for several seconds before saying, 'I know I look like your son, Mrs Major, but what is this all about? Why do you want to see me? Just to satisfy your curiosity? Though I must admit I'm curious too—about Luke. It's weird being told there's someone else who looks like me.'

'What I have to tell you,' smiled Helen, 'might seem even weirder still. Please come in.'

They followed her into Luke's study and there for the first time the two men faced each other. Luke of course, as Taryn had expected, betrayed no emotion, but Mark shook his head in bewilderment as though up till now he had not really accepted what he had been told and was having difficulty in believing his own eyes. 'It's not possible,' he said. 'I'd never have thought that——' He put a hand to his brow and looked round at the others, a perplexed smile playing on his lips.

Taryn thought Luke might have said something, but instead he remained aloof and dignified, almost as though he did not want to know his brother. It was excusable after a lifetime apart, but most men in his position would be overjoyed at the prospect of a new-found relative—especially someone as close as Mark.

Helen appeared not to notice Luke's reaction and bade them both sit down. 'First of all,' she said, looking directly at Mark, 'I want to ask you what might seem a perfectly irrelevant question, though I can assure you I have a very good reason for wanting to know.' She paused a moment. 'Are your parents still alive?'

To say Mark was surprised would be putting it mildly. He clearly had no idea why she should require such information and his eyes opened wide as he stared at her. 'No, they're not,' he managed to get out at last. 'They died when I was a lad—but what has that got to do with——'

'I'm coming to that, my boy, don't be hasty. If you had said they were alive it would have been improper for me to tell you what I have to say. It would have been your mother's responsibility. Has she ever told you the conditions of your birth?'

Still mystified, Mark shook his head. 'I know I was born in London—in not very wealthy circumstances, I might add—and I was glad to get away once I was old enough. What else is there to know?'

'Your mother adopted you,' Helen stated baldly, 'just as——'

'Hey, hang on,' he broke in. 'How do you know? I mean, we're complete strangers. Mark Vandyke's not even my real name.'

'It's only the surname that's different?' queried Helen, showing no sign at all of strain. Taryn surmised that only the initial shock had brought on her first attack and now that she was used to the idea of Luke meeting his twin, and especially as Luke himself had shown no sign of distress when discovering that she was not his real mother, she was enjoying the situation.

'That's right. I saw no reason to change Mark, but Jones—it was hardly suited for the world of fashion, wouldn't you agree?'

'If you say so,' agreed Helen mildly, 'though I'm afraid I've not yet discovered what you do for a living, and as it's hardly relevant in these circumstances, we'll leave that for later. No, I'm quite sure that you are the right man. We only have to look at you both together to dispel any doubts. I adopted Luke too, you know.'

'What she's trying to tell you,' butted in Luke impatiently, 'is that we're twins. Separated at birth, adopted by different families and consequently neither of us aware of the other's existence.'

Mark's mouth fell open and he jumped to his feet, again looking round at the other occupants of the room. 'Is this some kind of joke? I've never heard anything like it.'

'Neither had I—until a few minutes ago,' added Luke drily, 'but I'm ready to believe my mother, if you are?'

Taryn had never seen Mark lost for words. Usually he was completely self-assured. Then suddenly they were laughing and shaking hands and embracing one another. Again Taryn felt an outsider and would have gone had she not caught Helen's eye and been beckoned to her side. 'I'm so relieved,' Helen breathed. 'The times I've imagined this very scene, yet dreaded their meeting in case it all went wrong. I don't feel that I've lost a son, but gained another.'

'I'm very pleased for you, Helen. I must admit it's been a bit of a shock for me too, but you've been wonderful. I was worried in case you had another attack, like the last time Mark was mentioned.'

'So you noticed? I think maybe that's what has been my trouble all along –worrying about them meeting and discovering the truth. Now I have nothing to upset me I think I'll be all right.'

Once the excitement had died down Helen insisted on Mark staying with them for the remainder of his time in England. 'I won't allow you to go anywhere else,' she said. 'You two must be impatient to find out all about each other, and what better way than living together? Besides, I rather fancy the idea of having two sons.'

Shortly afterwards Taryn left, after promising Helen that she would return with her aunt for a celebration supper. She wanted to refuse, but knowing that Helen would be hurt if she did, and guessing that Gammy would enjoy the occasion anyway, she had reluctantly agreed.

She was right. Gammy was entranced by the whole situation, especially the fact that Luke and Mark were twins. 'Has it altered Luke's attitude towards you?' she asked.

'He hardly spoke to me,' admitted Taryn, 'though I don't blame him in all the excitement. I'd like to think that this will change things between us, but somehow I don't think it will. He's made up his mind that I love Mark, and the fact that he's proved to be his brother will probably make matters worse. There'll be a sense of honour involved now.'

'Poor Taryn, but I'm sure everything will turn out well in the end. Luke's had a disappointment. It will take time for him to get over it. Once he sees you really aren't in love with Mark any more he'll come back to you, never fear.'

Taryn was not convinced and for the rest of the day tried to think up an excuse for staying away from Dale End. It could only bring unhappiness as far as she was concerned, even though it was a unique occasion.

About an hour before they were due to go Mark returned for his things. He entered the room and swung Taryn round exultantly. 'Say, this is a turn-up for the book! When I came over here to make you my wife I never expected to find a brother as well. I really am in luck.'

Taryn waited until he had put her down before saying stiffly, 'I'm glad you think so.'

His lips pulled down wryly at the corners. 'You don't sound very happy. I guess things didn't go the way you wanted this morning. It's funny he didn't say anything to me about you, though come to think of it, we didn't have much time. We've been too busy reliving our youth.'

Taryn deliberately changed the subject. 'Are you and Luke going to try and find your real mother?'

'I don't think so,' his face suddenly serious. 'We're both of the same mind. If she didn't want us when we were babies she'd hardly be pleased to see us now. Helen says I can have a home with them whenever I want it. She's a great person, isn't she?'

'Delightful. Luke's been very lucky.'

'And now I'm to share in his luck. Oh, well, I must be off. Get myself ready for tonight. See you later.'

'I'm not coming.' The words were out before Taryn could stop them. 'Please give Helen my apologies, tell her I have a headache.'

He frowned. 'I don't believe you. You're making excuses.'

'Of course she is.' Gammy entered the room and looked severely at Taryn. 'You can't get out of it like that. Running away from a problem never solved anything. She'll be there, Mark, now off with you while we get ready.'

CHAPTER NINE

THE evening was the ordeal Taryn had expected. Luke ignored her completely whereas Mark was, if possible, more attentive than ever. It made no difference that she tried to ignore him, even rebuff him. He seemed intent on making everyone believe that Taryn was his girl, and Luke, if no one else, was convinced.

It was a relief when Gammy suggested they go home, though Taryn slept little and woke the next morning with heavy shadows beneath her eyes and a dull ache in the region of her heart. As she rode Dainty at full gallop across the moors she knew the time had come to leave the valley once more. The very place where she had sought solace had now become hell on earth. Through her brother she had heard of a job in London. Tomorrow she would write.

Mark was at the cottage when she returned. 'How about a spin out to the seaside?' he asked, taking one look at her wan appearance. 'You look as though you could do with a breath of sea air.'

Taryn shrugged. She didn't really want to go, but on the other hand it would be better than sitting at home all day. As Gammy had gone out Taryn left her a note and shortly afterwards they set off.

There was no picnic lunch with Mark. They

stopped after they had been on the road for an hour and he took her into a first-class restaurant. Taryn made a pretence of eating, but every mouthful choked her and in the end she put down her knife and fork and pushed away her plate. 'I'm sorry,' she said, 'I'm not hungry.'

'I don't understand you,' said Mark. 'Luke's made it perfectly clear that he no longer wants you—I wish you'd stop brooding. You have me. You loved me once, so why not again?'

Why not indeed? There was little likelihood of her reconciling her differences with Luke. He had made up his mind and that was the end of it. He would steer clear of Honeysuckle Cottage in future and Taryn was equally determined never to visit Dale End. His contempt was more than she could stand. She forced a smile. 'Maybe you're right. I don't know what to think any more.'

'Then let me do the thinking for us both, darling. Once you're used to having me around you'll soon discover that you're as happy as you were with Luke. In any case, you won't be losing him—for when we're married he'll be your brother-in-law. We'll be one big happy family.'

If anything had been a deterrent for keeping her from marrying Mark, this was. She wanted to get away from Luke altogether, not bring herself nearer to him. 'You're taking a lot for granted,' she said coolly. 'Who's said anything about marriage?'

'You'll come round to it in the end,' came the airy reply. 'Meanwhile let's enjoy ourselves.'

He took her to Torquay, not a place Taryn liked

very much. She preferred quiet, more out-of-the-way places, but on the whole it was a pleasant day. She had certainly come more to terms with herself by the time they reached home.

Her days followed a similar pattern after that. Each morning Mark arrived, to suggest they go out for a ride. As he was shortly to go back to Italy Taryn did not object. It was the first time he had visited England since he was a youth and there was no sense in spoiling his enjoyment by her own unhappiness. She did her best to hide her feelings, to such an extent that Mark seemed very sure of the fact that she would eventually marry him, and talked of the time when they would go back to Italy and set up home together.

Taryn had given up telling him that she had no intention of becoming his wife, though there were times when she succumbed to his kisses with no resistance at all. It was so easy to pretend he was Luke; just as in the beginning she had thought Luke was Mark.

The day of reckoning came when Mark declared he could stay in England no longer. 'I must get back to Italy soon,' he said after driving back to the cottage one night. 'I never meant to stay this long. Another week is the most I can manage. Will that be long enough for you?'

Taryn's eyes widened. 'For what?'

'To get your trousseau ready, of course. I take it you want to be married from here?' He patted his pocket. 'I have a special licence all ready.'

'Then I'm afraid you're going to be disappointed. Do I have to spell it out to you, Mark? For the last

172

time, I'm not going to marry you.'

'You don't still love Luke? After the way you've behaved these last few days I thought——'

'You thought you'd won,' cut in Taryn. 'I'm sorry if you feel let down, but it really is all over.'

'But you acted as though—you still cared. Taryn, please, don't joke with me, this is important.'

Taryn forced a smile at his crestfallen expression. 'To me too, that's why I can't marry you. I'm still fond of you, and I'll never forget all you've done for me, but it's Luke I love.'

'Despite the way he's treated you? I mean, if a fellow can't believe his girl when she tries to tell him the truth he's not worthy of her.'

Taryn shrugged. 'I can't help the way I feel. I'll always love him, no matter what.'

'You once said that to me.'

'I know, but this is different. I think that in Italy I was in love with the idea of being in love and didn't know my own feelings. Now I do—and although it looks as though I shall never find happiness with Luke I can't settle for second best with you.'

Mark sighed. 'You certainly don't pull any punches, but I'm not giving up yet. For your sake I hope brother Luke comes to his senses before too long, but don't forget I'll be waiting should you ever change your mind.' He gave a sudden and unexpected smile. 'Would you like me to put in a word for you?'

'Don't you dare! I'm not going to beg. As a matter of fact I'm leaving the valley. I've as good as got a job in London. I'm only waiting for confirmation.'

'Running away?' with a slight lift of his brows.

'Will it help?'

'The work will.' It was what she needed right now
—work, work and more work.

The next day Taryn received the expected letter.
It was a similar job to the one she had done at Dale
End and she was to start the following Monday. The
week passed slowly, still with no sign of Luke, although she knew he had not left Dale End. One half
of her wanted to stay; to make one last effort to
convince him that she had been telling the truth; but
the saner, more practical side of her knew the futility
in such a plan. If he had wanted to patch things up
between them he would have sought her out. It
proved that he did not truly love her.

Mark too appeared to have resigned himself to the
fact that Taryn wanted nothing more to do with him.
They still saw each other, but on a strictly platonic
basis. He offered to drive her to London on Saturday
as he was flying back to Italy on that day. She had
arranged for him to pick her up at eleven and was
surprised when he appeared two hours earlier.

'Helen wants to say goodbye,' he explained. 'She's
very disappointed you've not been up to see her.'

'Is Luke there?' was Taryn's instant response.

Mark shook his head. 'He's gone out for the day.'

'Does he know I'm leaving, as well as you?'

'Well—yes, I did tell him.'

He looked guilty, thought Taryn, so she said,
'Don't worry, I wanted him to know.' But it hurt that
he was going out of his way to avoid her. Did he hate
her so much that he couldn't even bring himself to
say farewell?

They found Helen in the lounge. When Taryn entered she immediately rose and held out her hands. 'My dear child, where have you been?'

Unwilling to meet the candid blue eyes, but having little choice, Taryn smiled wryly. 'I thought you'd understand.'

'Indeed I do, or at least I'm trying to, although in all honesty I must confess that I'm a little hurt by your behaviour.'

Taryn frowned. This wasn't the reaction she had expected. What did Luke's mother want her to do—beg his forgiveness even though Taryn herself had done no wrong? 'I'm sorry you feel like that,' she said, 'but don't you think that Luke's as much to blame?'

Helen lifted her shoulders tiredly and let them drop. 'Initially perhaps, in the heat of the moment, but if you'd given him time I'm sure things would have sorted themselves out.'

'Time?' echoed Taryn, astounded. 'How much did he want?' Helen had been so sympathetic the day it all began—why was she acting so strangely now? What had Luke said to her?

'A little more than you were prepared to give,' concurred Helen sadly. 'I'm sorry it turned out like this, sorry too that you're going away. Look after her, Mark.'

'I will, never fear.' He stepped forward and pulled Taryn's hand through his arm, giving her a sympathetic grin as he did so. 'Shall we go, darling? We don't want to rush.'

Taryn thought he was being a trifle familiar, especially in front of Luke's mother, but she returned his smile.

'All the best to you both,' said Helen, and to Taryn alone, 'I hope you know what you're doing.'

'It's the only way,' replied the young girl. 'Give my regards to Luke. It's a pity he's not here. I would like to see him again before I go.'

Helen shook her head. 'That would really be rubbing salt in the wound. Goodbye, my dear.'

All the way back to the cottage Taryn pondered over Helen's peculiar attitude. There was something she didn't understand. It was almost as though Helen thought she was going away with Mark. 'I can't weigh Helen up,' she said at last, unable to keep her thoughts to herself any longer. 'Why did she ask you to look after me? Anyone would think I was travelling to Italy with you.'

'You could do that. I'm sure you'd be much happier and there would certainly be no chance of bumping into Luke as you may well do here.'

'Maybe not, but you'd be a constant reminder. No, Mark, I won't change my plans now.'

It was not until later that she realised he had not answered her question; but she did not pursue the matter. What was the point? The whole affair had been one complete mystery right from the beginning. There had always been so much she did not understand—and now it looked as though she never would.

Gammy was upset by Taryn's decision to leave, and although up until now she had kept her own counsel she made one last-minute effort to try and dissuade her niece from going. 'I'm sure you're not doing the right thing,' she said. 'Give it a little longer. Once Mark's gone things will be different.'

Taryn hugged her aunt. 'Gammy, it's no use. I've got to go, even if only to sort out my own mind.'

'You still love Luke?'

She nodded. 'I always will. There'll never be anyone else for me.'

'The power of the rainbow.' Gammy's words were no more than a whisper, but Taryn heard, and understood, even if she did not fully agree.

After promising to keep in touch Taryn climbed into Mark's car. He had the engine revving up and a cloud of dust accompanied their exit from the valley. When Taryn looked back Dale End was obliterated from view. She was saddened by the thought of leaving behind that beautiful house. The many hours she had spent restoring it to its present splendour had endeared it to her heart—there had been a time when she had even visualised living there herself. That was before Luke . . . She tossed her head impatiently. What was the use in dreaming about what might have been? It was over. She must push it completely from her mind.

Mark too seemed absorbed by his thoughts and for the first hour the journey passed in silence. They stopped for lunch, but the restaurant was crowded and they had little opportunity for private conversation. Taryn felt that Mark was worrying about something, but put it down to the fact that his mind was now back on his business. It was unusual for him to be so absorbed in his thoughts, but Taryn was relieved, for she had feared he might persist in his efforts to try and induce her to accompany him to Naples. Afraid too that she might weaken, because he could be very persuasive when he tried.

They were held up in holiday traffic and by the time they reached London Mark was unable to take Taryn to her destination as he had previously planned. 'There's still time for you to change your mind,' he said urgently. 'Please, Taryn, I love you very much.'

But Taryn shook her head. 'No, Mark, don't——' Oh, God, why did they look so alike? Why wasn't it Luke declaring his love? She felt the prick of tears and swallowed quickly. 'Goodbye, hurry now or you'll miss your plane,' and she was out of the car before he could say any more.

She watched until he was out of sight and then the tears fell unchecked. Oh, Luke, Luke, she whispered, why have you done this to me? Why do you persist in misunderstanding? She stepped off the pavement, oblivious to the sound of traffic, not really knowing whether she was going in the right direction, sure only of the fact that this was the end of any chance of happiness, her life too for that matter, for what was the use of going on? Life without love was like flowers without rain; it could not survive— soon it would wither and die.

When the car hit her Taryn was oblivious to the pain, grateful only for the release from her misery. She knew not that she was taken to hospital, or that for several days she lay unconscious while a struggle went on to save her life. On the fifth day she opened her eyes to a sea of blurred faces. Her mouth felt dry and her head ached when she tried to lift it from the pillow.

A cool hand touched her brow and a gentle voice said, 'Please don't try to move. You've been very ill, but you're going to ...' The voice faded into oblivion.

The next time Taryn woke there was no one beside her bed. It was dark, the ward dimly lit. She struggled to remember what had happened. She had been crying. Why was she crying? Mark! He was involved—he had brought her to London—they had parted. Parted! It was Luke from whom she had parted. Luke. *Luke*.

Taryn did not realise she had called his name aloud until a figure emerged from the shadows of her room. 'You're awake at last?' A smiling nurse appeared in her line of vision.

By this time Taryn's memory had returned all too clearly. She looked at the nurse accusingly. 'Why didn't you let me die? I don't want to live without Luke. I don't want to——'

The nurse smoothed her brow and murmured soothingly as one would to a child. 'Tell me all about Luke. You've mentioned his name many times. Is he your boy-friend?'

'No, no.' Taryn tossed her head in anguish, stilled only by a rush of pain. 'He doesn't love me—he hates me.'

'You've had a quarrel?' comprehension lit the nurse's face. 'Never mind. I'm sure it can all be sorted out.'

'You don't understand.' Taryn sank back wearily

179

into the pillows. 'Nobody understands. Oh, why didn't you let me die?'

'It's our job to save lives,' insisted the nurse patiently. 'You won't feel like this once you're better. Would you like a drink?'

Taryn slowly shook her head. 'I think I'll go back to sleep.' Only then would she be free of the pain and heartache.

The sun filled the small ward with a golden light. It hurt Taryn's eyes and she closed them again quickly. Instantly a blind was drawn and she became aware of a figure standing beside her bed. The doctor was young and eager. He sat on the smooth pink covers and took her wrist between his fingers, consulting his watch as he did so. 'Hello there, Miss X. You've given us a bit of a fright. What's it all about, eh? It's a very serious thing to try and take your own life.'

Taryn's eyes widened. 'I didn't! What gave you that idea?'

'Nurse said you——'

'Oh, that,' tossed the girl. 'I *did* want to die, but I didn't purposely try to—to end it all,' and with a flash of humour, 'I'm sure I'd have done the job better if I had.'

He smiled and his grey eyes were kind. 'That's better. Not feeling so blue now? Suppose you tell us all about yourself. Your name, for instance. We can't go on calling you Miss X.'

'Taryn Penreath,' she submitted. 'How long have I been here?'

'Nearly a week.'

'Oh, gosh!' Taryn suddenly sat upright, disregarding the pain in her head. 'I was supposed to be starting a new job. Whatever will they think?'

'I'm afraid you won't be doing any work for some time yet, but if you'd care to give us your employer's name and address we'll make sure he knows the position. But don't you think it's more important to get in touch with your family? You're very much of a mystery. There was nothing in your handbag to tell us who you were. And the police have no trace of a missing person fitting your description.'

'Of course—my case, it's in Mark's car,' forgotten in her haste to escape.

'Mark? Who is he—your boy-friend?'

'Luke's brother. He gave me a lift.'

'Isn't it strange he's not tried to find you to bring back the case?'

'Not really. He was flying to Italy that same day, taking the car with him. He probably didn't notice until he got back.'

'But he would try to contact you?'

Taryn shugged. 'I suppose so, though he didn't know my address in London.'

'Surely you have a home. Where is that?'

'South Devon. I live with my aunt. She'll be wondering why I haven't written, though she won't worry—not yet. She'll assume I've been too busy.'

'And this man Luke. Nurse says you've quarrelled, yet his name was constantly on your lips. Would you like us to notify——'

'Oh no, not him. I don't want him here. He wouldn't come anyway,' she finished lamely.

'I'm sure you're misjudging him. If he loves you he'll come, whether you've quarrelled or not.'

'Not Luke. He thinks I love Mark.'

'And do you?' with an inquiring life of his brows.

'No. I did once, but not any more.'

'It sounds very complicated,' said the doctor, shaking his head, 'but I suppose you know what you're doing. Now, if you'll just give me the address of your aunt we'll notify her you're here. I expect she'll want to come and see you.'

'I'd prefer her not to know,' said Taryn firmly. 'You see, we live in a very small valley, no news is private, and I don't want Luke to find out. How much longer will I be here?'

'A few days, could be longer, depends on your progress.'

'Then leave it and I'll write to her as soon as I'm out.'

The doctor looked doubtful. 'We can't force you to tell us, but I'm not sure you're doing the wisest thing.'

'I am, I am—please try to understand.' Taryn caught the white-coated arm imploringly, her eyes big and bright, her lips parted anxiously.

He could not resist. He smiled and relented. 'Very well, though if you have to stay here any longer than three more days I'm going to insist you give us her address.'

Once Taryn showed signs of improvement she was moved into the main ward. She was very much the central figure as her mysterious arrival had caused great speculation throughout the hospital. Even now her refusal to disclose her whereabouts to her family was a point for much discussion, though Taryn herself declined to join in.

She was relieved when on the afternoon of the third day the doctor told her she was fit enough to leave. 'Now you must promise me that you won't do anything silly,' he said. 'Where do you intend going—back to Devon?'

'Not yet. I'll go and see if my job's still there first. You did tell them about my accident?'

He nodded. 'But I've no idea what their reaction was. In any case, I don't think you're fit enough for——'

'It's a very light job,' insisted Taryn. 'It won't tire me.'

She felt strange on leaving hospital, dressed in the clothes in which she had left the valley, neatly pressed and laundered, carrying only her handbag. She had a little money, but her cheque book and everything else was inside her case. Why she had put them there she did not know, but it was no use worrying about that now.

Her job was at a large house in Knightsbridge, redesigning the interior as she had done at Dale End. She took a taxi, but as it pulled up before the house her heart sank. It was an old grey building, one of a row all the same. Ugly in design, it did not even faintly inspire her. Nevertheless she paid the taxi driver and mounted the steps to the front door. A burly, florid-faced man answered her knock. She explained who she was, but even before she was half way through he said, 'I'm sorry, we've found some-one else. We expect punctuality, not a person who——'

'But I had an accident, didn't the hospital explain? I've only been discharged today.'

'I do remember something of the sort,' he said gruffly, 'but you're too late now, the job's gone. Good day to you.'

The door shut in her face and Taryn stood motion-less for a few seconds unable to believe that she had heard him correctly. She felt a childish urge to kick the door before swinging round on her heels and almost running down the steps.

Tears were not far away. She had relied on this job to get her away from Luke, and now she had no option but to return to Honeysuckle Cottage. She certainly hadn't enough money to stay in London for more than one night, even so it would leave her with only just enough for her train fare. She could go home now, of course, but wanted to ward off the evil hour for as long as possible. The thought of meeting Luke again and seeing the cold condemnation on his face was more than she could stand. It crossed her mind that he might have left by now, but there was no way of finding out until she got there.

Blindly Taryn walked street after street, not realising that she was not so strong as she used to be until her legs buckled beneath her and violent pains shot through her head. Leaning against a wall for support, she glanced anxiously round, not wishing anyone to see her plight. She need not have worried. Everyone was too intent on going their own way to notice the pale, tired girl who had almost reached the end of her tether. Unlike Ferndale, where everyone stopped to pass the time of day, London was an impersonal place, full of people yet more lonely than anywhere she had ever known. The cheerful sign of a hotel across the road attracted her attention. She would stay the night there and tomorrow make her way back to her Devonshire valley.

The receptionist gave her a funny look when Taryn announced that she had no luggage. However, she was shown to a small but clean room and after lying down for a few minutes on the superbly sprung bed Taryn felt much better. Rather than spend the whole evening alone in her room she went downstairs to the restaurant and although she did not feel hungry, once the meal was put before her and the tantalising smell of roast lamb and mint sauce reached her nostrils she developed a healthy appetite.

She lingered over her coffee, loth to go back to her room—and her thoughts. Here she was able to absorb herself in the atmosphere, pretend she was a member of the laughing party at the next table, or was being wined and dined by the handsome man across the other side. Her eyes scanned the room, almost missing the dark-suited man in the corner. He had his back to her, but there was something about him that drew her eyes back to look more closely at the brown hair curling close to his head.

Her heart missed a beat. It was all imagination. There were a thousand and one men who could look like Luke—or Mark—from behind. However, she could not refrain from staring in his direction, and almost as though he was aware of her interest he turned. Taryn ran the tip of her tongue across suddenly dry lips and averted her eyes. It *was* Luke. She could tell that by his conventional suit—but an unchanged Luke. The look he directed at her held no warmth. It was critical and faintly puzzled, but with no pleasure.

Taryn's eyes were once again drawn involuntarily towards his corner. He had risen and was making his way towards her. Her heart raced. She must go—before he made a scene—but her legs felt as though they were made of lead. It was like a bad dream when you scream for help but no sound comes. She couldn't move. Resolutely she looked down at the table, toying with the spoon in her saucer.

He was at her side. 'May I join you?' Cool and impersonal, he might have been talking to a stranger.

Taryn indicated the chair opposite and carried on playing with her spoon.

'Did you want to see me?'

She looked up then, a swift frown creasing her brow. 'What do you mean? How did I know you'd be here?'

'But you hoped I would, is that it?'

'What *are* you talking about?' asked Taryn, beginning to feel annoyed.

'Don't say you didn't know this was one of my hotels? What's the matter—brother Mark dropped you already and now you're trying to ingratiate yourself back with me?'

Taryn stiffened. 'As a matter of fact I didn't. If I

had I wouldn't be here, and as far as Mark's concerned he's gone back to Italy, as you well know. Now, if you'll excuse me——' She pushed back her chair, intent on escaping before he said any more horrid things calculated to hurt her.

But her wrist was caught in a vicelike grip. 'There are one or two matters I want clearing up first.'

'Really?' Taryn raised her brows disdainfully. 'I can't think what they might be. I thought you knew everything.'

His eyes narrowed at her unusual sarcasm. 'Not quite, but we can't talk here. We'll go to my office.'

But Taryn did not want to be alone with him. It was clear he still thought she was involved with Mark and she could only foresee more heartache by submitting herself to his questions. She rose, but once they were out of the restaurant darted for the stairs. It was unlikely that Luke would follow. After all, it was hardly fitting for the owner of the hotel to be seen running after a girl.

By the time she reached her room Taryn felt exhausted—a reminder that she was still far from well—and threw herself face downwards on the bed. She fought back the tears that welled, clenching her fists and cursing this quirk of fate that had brought her face to face with Luke. Her attempt at running away had failed miserably, and the fact that he thought she was here with the express purpose of trying to see him must have lowered her even further in his opinion.

I must go, she thought, leave the hotel before he tries to speak to me again. Dragging herself from the bed and without stopping to smooth her tousled hair, she picked up her handbag and opened the door.

The corridor was empty. Her feet faltered as she made her way along its length; her heartbeats quickened and breathing became more difficult. As she crept down the stairs Taryn broke out into a cold sweat; pausing for a second to regain her strength. Her legs felt as though they were made of cotton wool, but she forced herself on, intent only on leaving. It was ironical that out of all the hotels in London she had chosen this one. She put out a hand to steady herself as her vision blurred—everything was going round. Luke's distorted face swam before her eyes. She warded him off with her hands. 'Go away,' she cried. 'Go away!'

'Taryn!' She was caught and held firmly, tangled hair was smoothed from her brow. 'Taryn darling, please calm yourself. I'm not going to hurt you. Please tell me what's wrong.'

Her vision cleared. She lay on a bed in a strange room—a man's room—the smell of tobacco in the air. Luke sat beside her, a strangely gentle smile softening his face. She frowned and closed her eyes, turning her head to one side. It was imagination. Luke hated her—he wouldn't smile, like that—as though he still . . .

'Please say something,' he urged. 'Are you ill?'

'What does it matter to you?' she asked grimly, refusing to look at him.

'A great deal,' he replied.

He sounded so sincere that Taryn jerked her head in his direction. 'You must be joking. You hate me.'

It was his turn to look surprised. 'Have I ever said that?'

'Not in so many words, but the way you've be-haved——'

'What did you expect under the circumstances?'

'You could at least have accepted my explanation.' She pushed herself to a sitting position and glared defiantly.

'I was too shocked to think coherently at first,' he said slowly. 'By the time I got round to thinking you could have been telling me the truth it was too late.'

Taryn frowned. 'What do you mean? You haven't even tried to discuss it again.'

'What was the point? I went down to the cottage the next morning fully prepared to admit I had mis-judged you, and what did I find? A note saying you'd gone out with Mark for the day.'

'So what? It wasn't a confession of my love.'

'No?' his eyebrows raised sceptically. 'That's not what Mark said.'

Suddenly everything began to fall into place. By taking her out every day Mark had made sure she didn't meet Luke again, didn't have the opportunity to clear up their misunderstanding. All the time Mark had been playing it his way—though it hadn't worked out entirely. He had not counted on the strength of Taryn's love for Luke. 'Exactly what has Mark told you?' she asked at length.

'You should know,' he responded drily. 'You've always loved him—you only turned to me because we were so alike. He said you didn't even want to see me again after he'd turned up and that you were going to get married when you got back to Italy.'

Taryn shook her head as if in a daze. 'Mark wouldn't treat me like that. It's not possible.'

Luke watched her closely. 'Where is he? Why are you here on your own?'

'He's in Italy as far as I know,' shrugged Taryn, 'and me—well, I had a job here, but I had an accident and they didn't keep it open. I'm going back home to-morrow.'

A flicker of hope shone in Luke's eyes. 'So you weren't going to Italy after all?'

Taryn shook her head. 'He wanted me to. He wouldn't believe I didn't love him any more. He tried, right to the end, I'll give him that.'

'But why did you leave the valley?' He caught her hands. 'Tell me, Taryn. It's important I know.'

She lowered her eyes, pulses racing at his touch. Swallowing painfully, she said, 'Because I couldn't bear the thought of meeting you—seeing the look of disapproval on your face——'

'Stop!' His own voice gruff with emotion. 'I can't bear it. Oh, Taryn,' he pulled her head down on to his shoulder and held her close until she thought she would suffocate. 'Taryn, I do love you. What a fool I've been! I ought to have known you wouldn't lie to me.'

'Never,' her tones muffled against his suit. 'Not to you, Luke.'

Suddenly he held her at arms' length. 'What am I thinking? What was this you said about an accident? You look far from well—are you sure you ought to be wandering around on your own?'

'I'm all right now,' Taryn assured him. 'It was after I'd left Mark—I was thinking of you, and didn't look where I was going—the next thing I knew I was in hospital. I was unconscious for nearly a week.'

'Oh, God! To think it's all my fault. You might have been killed. Why didn't they send for me—or Gammy at least?'

'They didn't know who I was, and when I did come round I wouldn't let them. I didn't want your sympathy, I wanted——' She stopped and looked at him.

'Yes?' he prompted softly.

'I wanted your love—as you have mine.'

Their lips met in a mutually satisfying kiss and the minutes ticked by as they gave themselves up to the wonder of their love.

There were still many questions left unanswered, but for the moment Taryn was content to remain in the arms of the man she had thought lost to her for ever. Today was indeed a wonderful day, and the power of Gammy's rainbow had proved itself in the end.

I wonder if Luke believes in rainbows? she thought. I must ask him—some time.